BARUN RAI AND THE HOUSE ON THE CLIFF

AND OTHER STORIES

Novelisation by Joe Hetherington
Based on the film *Barun Rai and the House on the Cliff*,
Written by Sam Bhattacharjee and Sara Bodinar

INDIA • SINGAPORE • MALAYSIA

ISBN 979-8-88909-990-1

BARUN RAI AND THE HOUSE ON THE CLIFF & OTHER STORIES

Novelisation by
JOE HETHERINGTON

Based on the film
BARUN RAI AND THE HOUSE ON THE CLIFF,

Written by
SAM BHATTACHARJEE AND SARA BODINAR

Based on Characters created by
SAM BHATTACHARJEE

Original Short Stories by
JOE HETHERINGTON

Illustrated by
CALLUM BENTLEY

In loving memory of David Bailie and Nilav

FOREWORD

By Priyanshu Chatterjee, titular star of

'Barun Rai and the House on the Cliff'.

FOREWORD

By Sara Bodinar

Sam and I have worked closely together for the past 6 years, on many different projects and when he first approached me about writing the script for 'Barun Rai And The House On The Cliff' I was instantly sold on the concept. Barun Rai is a parapsychologist detective sent to investigate a series of paranormal crimes taking place in the sleepy English village of Corvid's Head during the late 1970s.

To research the character I studied the many historical news reports regarding ghost sightings along the coastline near Beachy Head on the British South Coast. We wanted to create a unique detective, who was both investigating crimes that were taking place in the supernatural realm, but also using the science of the time to find clues.

Much of the film was shot in a farmhouse in the sprawling Romford countryside, just outside London. It was isolated, and eerie, perfect for creating an unsettling mix of old-fashioned ghost story and modern, sophisticated horror. We wanted to play with the emotions of the audience in new, compelling and memorable ways. This book is an extension of that.

Ultimately Barun Rai is a tough nut and an enigma. It feels like nothing will ever phase him, not even the severity of the symptoms he experiences when he becomes part of a ghostly underworld. We wanted the audience to be drawn to his charms, as well as his vulnerabilities. I hope you enjoy the book as much as we enjoyed writing the film.

BARUN RAI AND
THE HOUSE ON THE CLIFF

CHAPTER ONE

Most of us can't see all that is around us. I see things others cannot. Often, I ask myself: is it a gift or a curse? After years of pondering the same question, I still do not know the answer.

This neighbourhood was a far cry from the affluent streets that encompassed it, despite the fact that the facades of all the buildings in this district were practically identical. Barun did not need anyone to show him the way to his destination. An intimidating alleyway led to a squalid block of apartments, the stench of overflowing drains thick in the air. Taking a drag of his cigar, Barun strode purposefully into the alley to be met with a cacophony of voices. There were spirits here. It was unusual to see so many dead men and women occupying such a small area, but then again, this was a perfect spot to conduct all manner of illicit activities. All of the spirits tried to catch his attention in one way or another, a majority merely wanting to intimidate him. Though he did not pay them the slightest notice as he breezed past the spectres, Barun did observe out of the corner of his eye that it appeared that none of them had been dead any longer than twenty years judging by their clothing. Why had there been so much death in such a short space of time?

The spirit who tried the hardest to gain his attention was a biker, Barun catching a whiff of oil as he strode past the dead man. Barun had only recently finished writing an essay on phantom aromas and how anyone, no matter how attuned they were to the spirit world, could detect these smells. Like most of his papers, many close-minded academics had been quick to ridicule it. Ducking under police tape, Barun was greeted by a portly man waiting in the lobby.

'Barun! Thank you again for coming,' the man said, slapping him on the shoulder.

Very nearly bald, Detective Cartwright had compensated for the lack of hair on his head by growing a bushy moustache that covered his top lip. Three of the fingernails on his right hand were missing, and the officer was quick to tell anyone who would listen that he had lost them through frostbite whilst on a particularly cold stakeout during a spell as an Alaskan state trooper.

'It has been too long, detective. Hopefully there'll come a day when we cross paths away from a crime scene.' Barun gestured at the tape.

'Yeah, I guess it's best we start talking business right away.' The detective hitched up his trousers, his gaze drifting to a flight of stairs. 'This is a real nasty one, my friend: murder-suicide. He burst into two apartments and killed four before turning his Colt on himself.'

'And I take it the killer did not know their victims?' Barun asked.

'That's right,' Detective Cartwright said. 'We have no idea who he was and where he came from. A colleague of mine mentioned you were in the country, and after how you came to my rescue in that drowning case in Chicago, I couldn't think of anyone better to call.'

'Well, I will try my best to shed some light on what happened.' Barun put his cigar out in a nearby ash tray that was upon a long disused desk. It appeared to him that this station had once been used by a doorman or an attendant of some other kind, though now it was little more than a graveyard for bugs.

'And that's all I can ask.' Cartwright gave a feeble smile. 'My chief's been on my back for days on this one. He wants the case shut by tonight. I can see his point as we know for sure who pulled the trigger, it's just that I sense there's something not right. There's been a helluva lot of deaths on this street in recent years. Some have been people you'd expect to get whacked sooner or later, like hoods and bookies, but there've been times we've turned up here to find some model student who's bit the big one. Strange thing is, all the other one's I can think of have also ended in the killer committing suicide.'

A young officer clumsily entered the lobby, dislodging the tape as he approached the two men.

'Heck, Rossi, you need to learn to be more careful.' Cartwright rolled his eyes. 'What is it?'

'Sorry, sir, it's just an APB has come through,' the young officer said, trying to catch his breath. 'There's been a shooting on fifth.'

Detective Cartwright let out an exasperated groan. 'Of course there has. I gotta go, Barun, but I think Detective Daniels is hanging around somewhere.'

'Don't worry about me.' Barun gave a wave of his hand. 'You best get going.'

The two policemen began to depart, though Cartwright had barely walked two steps before he clicked his fingers and turned around. 'I forgot to say: rooms three and five.'

Barun nodded. 'Thank you.'

Once the officers had taken their leave, Barun ascended the staircase, and as he did, he perceived a drop in temperature. A sharp pain then shot through his head, and he grabbed the railing to steady himself. Screams could be heard coming from somewhere in the building. Wiping his forehead with the back of his hand, Barun headed towards the noise and was unsurprised to find that it was emanating from one of the rooms that Cartwright had mentioned.

Even more dilapidated than the hallway, the apartment was shabby and its walls were so heavily damaged that in places it was possible to see straight into the cavities. Within seconds of entering the crime scene, a vision came to Barun. The killer stood before him. Bald and around half a foot shorter than Barun, the man was unassuming and his appearance was not that of a archetypal murderer. A glazed look in his eyes, the man pulled the trigger of his pistol and gunned down the first of his victims. Another scream rang out as the partner of the victim begged in vain for her life.

Barun walked through the scene, studying each detail. The accuracy that the killer displayed with his weapon suggested that he had some experience using a firearm.

Meanwhile, though it was not unusual for a murderer to show little in way of emotion, there was something greatly amiss with the blank look on the man's face. Barun's vision swiftly drew him away from the room, and he wandered into the next apartment. These people had heard the gunshots and screams through the walls. Fear and confusion had already taken a hold of them by the time the killer knocked down their front door with a single kick. He shot his weapon the moment he stepped over the threshold, killing a woman where she stood. Cowering, his final victim meekly raised his hands as a bullet pierced his chest.

At last, Barun heard her. In a voice that was both soft and beguiling, she told the killer to walk into the bedroom. Her dominance over him was so strong that he did not hesitate when she issued her final command.

'Kill yourself,' she whispered.

With her host dead, the spirit rose from the body and glowered at Barun. Her face was etched in unbridled fury, and she wore a sodden gown which was tattered at the hem. She let out a terrible shriek as the vision began to fade away. Drained from the experience, Barun slumped into a chair, the last gunshot still ringing in his ears. An image of a portrait within a dank room flashed into his mind. There then came a blinding light, and a deep serenity descended over him. Everything was pieced together in a blink of an eye, and he sat in quiet contemplation as he mulled over his findings.

It took him a while to realise that there was a police officer standing in the doorway watching him with wide eyes.

'Are you okay, sir?' the officer asked, his voice wavering.

Barun looked around the room. Gone entirely were the echoes of the past, blood stains the only indication of the horrors that had taken place.

'I am fine. Thank you for asking.' Barun gave a weak smile. 'Am I correct that there is a Detective Daniels on the scene?'

'Yeah, you are.' The officer raised an eyebrow. 'There's a foyer on the top floor. You wait up there and I'll go fetch her.'

Barun followed the officer's instruction and waited in the dingy foyer by himself for some time. He had not expected the detective to be so young. A diminutive figure, Detective Daniels had a complexion as pale as milk and a tense jaw. Over her shoulder was slung a brown satchel. Striding into the foyer, she inspected Barun as though he was a suspect in a police lineup. Barun rose from the threadbare chair that he had been sitting on to greet her.

'You must be Cartwright's specialist.' She sneered. 'What do you want?'

'My name is Barun Rai, and I have information that is useful to your investigation,' he said, sitting back down.

Daniels rolled her eyes before taking a seat opposite to him. 'I don't know what Cartwright's told you, but there is no investigation. Some sick loner broke into an apartment with a gun. We have the murder weapon, the killer's in the morgue and for good measure we have a witness who saw him entering the building. All in all, the case is as good as closed.'

'Detective Cartwright told me, however, that you did not know the man's identity.' Barun intertwined his fingers.

'Right.' Detective Daniels shuffled uncomfortably in her seat. 'Another precinct had picked him up a few weeks back for swiping a pack of cigarettes from a convenience store, but he gave them an alias as well as a fake address. All we got from them that was remotely useful was his mugshot.' The detective reached into her satchel and pulled out a sheet.

Taking the photograph, Barun looked into the eyes of the man who he had seen in his vision. 'His real name was Troy Latchman,' Barun said. 'Born in Houston in the summer of 1951, he spent most of his life in the city and was imprisoned in a penitentiary as a young adult.'

Detective Daniels stared incredulously at him. 'And how the heck do you know all that? Let me guess, you're a psychic?'

Barun let out a brief laugh before speaking. 'Well, I am a criminal investigator by title, though I deal with cases that are. . . out of the ordinary.' He paused a moment. 'I appreciate that this may sound absurd to you, but Troy Latchman did not intend to kill these people. I saw something. . . I saw someone. It was a girl. She made him do it.'

'So you're telling me he was possessed by a ghost? That's some imagination you've got there.' She curled her lip. 'You know, my patience is growing thinner with every word that comes out of your mouth. If you don't give me something concrete in the next ten seconds, I'm going to have you arrested for trespassing.'

'There is a picture of her in the basement,' Barun said coolly.

'How did you get into the basement?' Daniels demanded. 'It's locked.'

'I never set foot in the basement.' Barun sighed. 'Look, if I don't find out who this girl was, you run the risk of this happening time and time again.'

Daniels' face softened ever-so-slightly. 'The janitor showed me in there before. He told me that she used to own this whole block, but she went missing over twenty years ago. That's all there is to know.'

'Please, I must inspect the room.' Barun leaned forwards in his seat. 'Ten minutes, that's all I need.'

'Fine.' The detective gave a stiff nod, taking a set of keys from her pocket. 'Ten minutes, then I want you gone.'

Barun had only had a fleeting glimpse of the basement, though he instantly recognised the tiny, barred window and, of course, the portrait. Within a brass frame covered in a layer of dust, the painting depicted a proud-looking woman wearing a cerulean gown. Detective Daniels started to reach out to brush away some of the dust from its plaque, but Barun quickly grabbed her wrist.

'I would not do that if I were you,' Barun said.

She pulled her arm away. 'Remember, ten minutes, Mister Rai.'

Scanning the room, it became quite clear to him that there was nothing he could learn from just looking around. Hesitation came over Barun. Though he knew what needed to be done, he was quite sure that it was going to be an altogether unpleasant experience for him.

After first taking a deep breath in through his nostrils, he crouched down and placed his palm to the floor. Instantly, pressure was exerted on his windpipe. A shadow stood above him, its hands wrapped around his throat. Though the woman in the portrait had been attacked on this spot, she had not died in this room. Two boulders leaned against each other. Both rocks had flecks of yellow paint upon them.

Rain was thrashing down relentlessly. Undeterred by the weather, a man wearing a trenchcoat was shovelling. With half her face pressing against ground, she had watched out of one eye as this man who would become her killer dug her grave. She had tried to say something as she lay there, but her voice was so weak that she could only mouth the word. Barun drew his hand back and started to gasp for air.

'W-what was that?' Daniels stammered, her mouth lolling open after she had finished speaking.

Giving his throat a rub, Barun got to his feet. 'She did not die in this building, but she maintains a spiritual link to this place through the painting. On the banks of the Hudson River, there are two very distinct boulders which lean into one another. That is where she is buried.'

Daniels furrowed her brow. 'These boulders don't happen to have a small amount of paint on them, right?'

'They do,' Barun said. 'Yellow paint.'

'Okay.' The detective went quiet for a while as she massaged her temple. 'Mister Rai, I want you to go back upstairs and wait for me there. I've got some calls to make.'

Returning to the chair he had been sat in at the foyer, Barun collected an ash tray and placed it on his knee. He had smoked his way through four cigars and was on the verge of falling asleep by the time the detective reappeared. Barun noticed that the cantankerous demeanour that Daniels had been exhibiting when they had first met was gone without a trace, and she was currently displaying an amicable expression upon her face.

'I have spoken to the sheriff over in Houston.' She brushed her hair back behind her ears as she sat down. 'He confirmed that a man named Troy Latchman was once arrested by his department for holding up a drugstore. The description he gave of him fits our mugshot. I have asked him to send up a copy of the picture that they had in his file to make sure, but it sounds like you were right, Mister Rai.'

'That is good to hear.' Barun nodded. 'And what of the murdered woman? Did you locate her?'

Daniels pursed her lips. 'I sent a few of our boys down to the river with some shovels. She was there, barely four feet under. The poor woman was right where you said she would be.'

Part of him wished he had been wrong; it was never a good feeling to be told that a body had been found.

'At least she is at peace now,' he said solemnly.

'Look, I'm not getting onboard with your ghost theory, but there is something I need to know: why would she kill these people having met such a violent end herself?' Daniels asked.

'Violence breeds violence.' Barun shrugged. 'Spirits see the world very differently to us. She would not have recognised the people she killed, and in her confusion she may have thought that she was enacting her revenge. Perhaps I should add, try not to judge the dead by mortal morals, detective.'

Daniels narrowed her eyes. 'You'll have to forgive me for having little sympathy for anyone who kills innocents. That in fact brings me to the last question I wanted to ask: do you know who killed her?'

'No,' Barun said. 'The vision I had in the basement was through the eyes of the woman, and it seemed that she had blocked the identity of her assailant from her mind before she passed.

Whoever it was, I sense that they were likely known to her.'

'Well, Mister Rai, it is my turn to reveal something,' Daniels said. 'A confession was left in an envelope with the body. They had not written much, though from what I gathered over the phone it seemed like greed was the motivation. They had signed the letter with the initials MB.'

Barun stared down at the floor. MB. In her final moments, she had attempted to plead with the man. Only now did Barun realise that the word she had tried to say was a name.

'Marcus,' Barun said, almost to himself.

'Are you sure?' Daniels asked.

Not looking to the detective, he gave a slow nod. 'Towards the end of my vision, I felt her mouth move as though it were mine. That was the word she was trying to say, I am certain.'

'I'll look into,' Daniels said. 'Not wanting to sound all pessimistic, but the chances of us actually bringing anyone to justice are low. Even if we do find out who the guy is, it's been such a long time since the crime was committed that it could be difficult to prosecute him even with a confession. That's if he's even still alive.' Daniels raised her hand as though she was swearing an oath. 'That said, it's now no longer a cold case, and I will be putting in a request with my superiors for me to be assigned to the investigation. While there are still leads to chase, I certainly won't be giving up.'

'I expect nothing less from you, detective.' Barun smiled. A powerful tiredness came over him, his shoulders feeling heavy. 'Sorry, today has taken a lot out of me, and I'm feeling rather worse for wear now. I should take my leave.'

After first laying the ash tray to one side, Barun stood up.

'Of course.' Detective Daniels also got to her feet. 'Thank you, Mister Rai. This whole experience has been. . . enlightening. Maybe there will come a time in the future when I'll be able to fathom what occurred here this day.'

'Even I after all my years of working in this field know but the tip of the iceberg.' Barun said, shaking her hand. 'I daresay that neither of us will ever come close to comprehending the spirit world. That is, until we have passed into that realm.'

Daniels screwed up her face. 'Are you always this macabre?'

'It is difficult to be anything but when you spend your life talking about the dead.' Barun shrugged.

CHAPTER TWO

It was happening again. Brian was yet to figure out the reason why he always knew when to make for the cliffs. There were no physical signs that it was about to take place, such as changes in the weather or strange behaviour from animals, it was just an urge that he would get when it was time.

Camera in hand, he crept down the stairs so as to not wake his mother who was asleep in front of the television set in the living room. He gently shut the front door behind himself before breathing in the sea air. On the horizon, the sun had only just dawned, and with the exception of the milkman who was delivering on the other side of the road, Brian was alone on the street. He liked the village this time of year; most of the seasonal tourists had departed, yet the temperature was mild and not yet autumnal. There was little to differentiate between Corvid's Head and any of the other villages located on the islands that surrounded mainland Britain: it was picturesque, there was a church at its centre and all the residents knew one another.

The cliffs were but a short walk from his home, and he was met with a familiar sight when he reached them. A solitary figure stood on the edge, peering down towards the rocks below. Inching closer, Brian readied his camera then took two pictures a few seconds apart from one another. First the man dangled his foot over the edge as if he was having second thoughts, then suddenly he sprang forwards. Just like it had been with the others, there was something unnatural in the way he leapt.

As the man plummeted to his death, Brian took a burst of pictures. He wiped his nose with his sleeve before proceeding down a nearby slope to get a better view. The tide had already washed away most of the blood by the time he reached the bottom. Placing the camera to his eye, Brian's finger hovered over the shutter button as he prepared to take one final picture of the man. It would not be his best work, he reckoned, but there was little he could do about the overbearing glare of the sun.

*

Jenny had only just placed her coat on the stand when her phone rang. A call this early in the morning was never good news. After first letting out an audible sigh, she picked up the receiver. 'This is Inspector Jones speaking.'

'Jenny, it's Kyle,' the man said in a distressed tone. 'There's been another one.'

Her breath catching in her throat, Jenny knew what he was referring to immediately.

Although she had only been the highest ranking officer in the village for three years, the number of people who had committed suicide by jumping from the cliffs had almost reached double figures during her time in charge. Despite the high number, her nine-strong police force was generally not well-accustomed to death. In the same space of time, there had not been a single murder on the island, and the majority of the crimes that they dealt with were petty ones, such as children stealing from sweet shops.

'Are you still there, Jenny?' Kyle asked.

'Yes, sorry,' she blurted out. 'Give me ten minutes.'

Hanging up the receiver, she grabbed her coat then made for the door. Word always spread quickly in the village. Jenny arrived to find that half of the local press were already milling around, and as soon as they caught sight of her Rover P6 pulling up, they all began to jog towards her. The questions started the moment that Jenny opened the door.

'Ladies and gentlemen, I would like you all to vacate the area,' she called as she brushed past them. 'I will be holding a press conference in an hour's time, but at present I have no comment.'

She was thankful that the journalists heeded her request, the crowd instantly starting to disperse. Continuing on, Jenny met up with one of her constables who was in deep conversation with a woman who was holding the reins of a horse.

'Inspector, I've just been interviewing Miss Ramshaw here.' Constable Atkins nodded towards the woman. 'She was out riding when she saw a man on the edge of the cliffs.'

'I did,' the woman confirmed in a timid voice. 'I could tell straight away that he was going to jump then. . . he was just gone.'

'And there was no one in the vicinity of him?' Jenny asked.

'There was. Not long after he fell, I noticed someone behind the thicket over there.' Miss Ramshaw pointed. 'I think it was that Dawson boy.'

Jenny exchanged a glance with Constable Atkins.

'Thank you for your time, Miss Ramshaw. We may need to speak with you again if that is alright.' Jenny gave a weak smile.

'Of course. You know where to find me,' the woman said as she mounted her horse. Jenny waited until she had ridden away before speaking.

'Kyle, can you go and pick up the boy?' she asked the constable. 'Find out if he took any pictures like last time.'

'Righto, Inspector. I'll see to that at once.' Constable Atkins nodded. 'The coroner and Stepney are on the shore. We're just waiting on the ambulance to collect the body.'

The walk down to the rocks was perilous as there were no handrails running along the slope. Around the midway point, a rock became dislodged under Jenny's foot, and she was forced to grab onto the cliff face to prevent herself from slipping. Slightly shaken from the experience, she proceeded with extra caution for the remainder of her descent.

Tall and barrel-chested, Sergeant Stepney stood vigil over the body, whilst the coroner was absent-mindedly pacing over the rocks with a cigarette hanging out of his mouth.

'Ma'am, we believe the deceased is Adrian Worthington, the chap who moved into that thatched house on the incline about ten months back,' the sergeant said, placing his hands behind his back. 'I've sent a couple of the lads round to collect his partner. Hopefully this ambulance gets here soon otherwise they might get to the morgue before us.'

A blanket was draped over the deceased, a bloodied arm protruding from under the covering. 'You have lived here your whole life, haven't you, sergeant?' Jenny asked, her eyes fixed on the body.

'That I have, ma'am.'

'Tell me, how many people have thrown themselves onto these rocks in that time?'

The sergeant puffed out his cheeks. 'Blimey, I don't know. Thirty? Probably more to be honest. They've all been residents of the village as far as I'm aware. No wonder there's a tall tale about the village being cursed.'

'Yes, quite,' Jenny murmured, craning her neck up to look at the cliff edge.

*

There were few things in life that Jenny disliked more than being interviewed: holding a press conference in front of cameras was one of them. The journalists had asked variations of the same question whilst Jenny had supplied variations of the same answer. Once the ordeal was over, she made straight for the station. The body had been confirmed as that of Adrian Worthington by the late man's fiancée. So shocked had she been when she had seen his face that the poor woman had fainted from shock. Meanwhile, the Dawson boy had handed over several photographs that he had taken of the man before and after his fall.

Upon inspection of the pictures, one of the constables found them disturbing enough to warrant an arrest, placing the boy in a cell. They had then been left in a brown envelope upon Jenny's desk. Sitting down, she took a deep breath before opening the envelope. Studying the first of them, Jenny felt her heart rate rise when she noticed an oddity in the picture. Behind the man there was a formless mass which was lingering as he peered down over the edge.

Quickly, she spread the photographs across her desk. In every single one, it was present. Although whatever the thing was appeared misty in the earliest pictures that had been taken, it seemed to have slowly taken shape as the tragedy had unfolded. Jenny leaned in closer. She could swear that she could see an opaque figure looming over the body. She could make out a pair of outstretched arms. An open mouth. Pale eyes.

There came a knock at the door which caused Jenny to jump. 'Come in,' she said authoritatively.

Opening the door ajar, Sergeant Stepney poked his head inside the room. 'Is it okay if we have a chat, ma'am?'

'Of course, Stepney. Take a seat.'

The man leisurely entered and sat opposite his senior officer. 'Bit of an unusual day, eh?'

'I do believe that that is an understatement, sergeant,' Jenny said, directing his attention to the desk. 'I'm under the impression you've already seen these. Anything appear off to you?'

Sergeant Stepney gave a cursory glance at the pictures. 'Take it that you're referring to those marks? Dirt on the lens by the look of it.'

'You're writing these off as dirt? Even this one?' she asked, pointing.

'Mind can play tricks on you, ma'am.' He folded his arms. 'I saw a cloud that looked like an elephant the other day; doesn't mean that there's a ghost elephant in the sky.'

Jenny pulled a face. 'Point taken, though you don't have to be so flippant about it.'

'Sorry, ma'am.' Stepney looked down at his feet.

Leaning back in her seat, Jenny rested her chin on her hand. 'Did Brian Dawson tell us why he was there with his camera?'

'Said he was going to take a snap of the sunset. Funny how he's been present for the past three suicides,' Stepney said. 'Then again, I suppose he does live a stone's throw away from the cliffs.'

'He certainly has a tendency to be in the wrong place at the wrong time.' Jenny furrowed her brow in thought. 'Phone his mother and ask her to come to collect him. Keep an eye on him though, sergeant. There's something amiss with that boy.'

'You can say that again,' Stepney mumbled under his breath.

'Was there anything specific that you wanted to discuss?' Jenny asked.

'Oh, yes. I came to tell you about the fiancée.' Sergeant Stepney opened his notebook. 'Unsurprisingly, we didn't get too much sense out of her. Apparently he'd been quite a jolly fellow up until about a week ago. She caught him in the garden sat in the dirt reading some grubby book. After that, he started disappearing in the middle of the night, and when he returned he seemingly had no recollection of where he had been. Sounded like sleepwalking to me at first, but she then explained that he was coming home fully dressed with his shoes caked in mud. The rest of what I got down is all rather vague; I'm not sure if you'll follow it.'

'Keep going.' Jenny gave an impatient gesture.

'Well she went on about some woman poisoning his mind.' Sergeant Stepney followed his notes with his finger. 'I asked her who this was, and she just looked blankly at me. When I pressed her, she gave me a shove in the arm then told me I'll never find her. In all honesty, it appeared like the shock had taken its toll by this stage.'

'Yes, it sounds like it.' Jenny started to place the pictures back in the envelope. 'If you don't mind, sergeant, I've got a call to make.'

'Certainly, ma'am.' He gave a respectful nod before leaving.

There was now only one picture that she had not returned to the envelope: the last photograph the boy had taken. She examined it once more. The sergeant was not even open to modern ideas of policing, so she was not surprised that he had been quick to reject the notion that something sinister may have been involved in the man's death. Ardent sceptics would, naturally, always ridicule those who believed in the supernatural. Unlike Jenny, these people had never seen something that could not be explained by science.

She had been a constable working in London when she had been asked to attend to a disturbance at a flat. Nothing could have prepared her for the scene she walked in on. The young woman causing the commotion was speaking in a gravelly voice, a man's voice, and she was cutting at her face with a kitchen knife. Acting quickly, Jenny had ordered the woman's family to leave the flat for their own safety, a move that had infuriated the distressed woman. With the individual's actions becoming progressively more aggressive, Jenny had started to fear for her own wellbeing. If he had not turned up when he had, she was not sure what she would have done. His name escaped her, but he had called himself a parapsychologist and was supported by a young man called Sukhbir. In desperation, the family had contacted these private investigators as well as the police.

The two men had quickly established that the woman had come in contact with a malevolent spirit that was possessing her body. Doors had begun to repeatedly slam on their own accord by this point, whilst an ornament flew off a shelf, narrowly missing Jenny. Using amulets and incense, he had somehow managed to calm the situation down before drawing a shadowy being from the woman. It had screeched and thrashed around the room upon leaving its host. Jenny had felt a deep hopelessness in the thing's presence, a sensation that had caused her to drop to the ground with her hands over her face. The parapsychologist then confronted it for the final time and, after he had spoken to it in an ancient tongue, the shadow had shrunk into nothingness.

Jenny opened the drawer of her desk and plucked her phonebook from it. She paused momentarily. Her superiors would never condone a private investigator with such unorthodox methods scouring the village. Then again, they were often uncontactable for weeks on end so there was a chance that they would not find out. Breathing out through her nose, Jenny opened the phonebook and found Sukhbir's number. The scribble had faded slightly, but it was still legible. It had been nearly ten years since she had taken down the man's contact details. Maybe he no longer lived at that address? And even if he did, was he still in the same line of work? Picking up the receiver of her telephone in one hand, she used the index finger of her other to start to turn the rotary dial.

CHAPTER THREE

Barun arrived back in London in plenty of time for his lecture. He had always found that New York and London had much in common: smog clung to the air in both places whilst the inhabitants of the two cities always seemed to be perpetually rushing around. The taxi ride to the university gave him a chance to mull through his notes. His audience were to be a group of undergraduates studying criminology, and this was to be the second occasion that he had given a talk at the university. The last time, the students that had attended had been far from impressed with his theories. He could only hope that today's crowd were not ones to heckle.

A member of the university's staff was waiting at the entrance hall for him. On a chain around her neck were a pair of spectacles, and her mouth was curled into a sullen pout. 'Mister Rai, yes?' she asked once he had paid his taxi driver.

'That is me.' Barun smiled.

'We have prepared a function room for you and set up a projector as you had asked,' she said, folding her arms. 'Follow me.'

Though the lady was only around three quarters of his height, Barun struggled to keep up with her. By the time they reached their destination, he was nearly out of breath.

'Here it is. If you need anything, I'll be on the third floor, ninth door on the right if you are heading up the main staircase.' The woman strode off the second she finished speaking.

'Thank you,' Barun called after her, though she was already out of his sight.

After he had loaded his film into the projector, Barun gave his notes a final glance before placing them in a neat pile upon a table which was by the screen. The room soon began to fill the students. Overall, his lecture appeared to go down relatively well with his audience. There were a few looks of incredulity in the opening stages which were then followed later by a chorus of gasps when he showed them footage of an exorcism that had been carried out in South America, but he nonetheless received a round of applause at the conclusion of his talk. A group of young women approached him afterwards, and asked him if they were doing something wrong in their séances as their efforts to contact the other side had so far been utterly fruitless. He remained very polite throughout the conversation, though the women were terribly ill-informed on the matter and some of the questions they asked bordered on being disrespectful.

He was packing away his belongings when he was told that there was a phone call for him. 'Hello, this is Barun Rai speaking,' he said unsurely into the phone.

'It's me, Barun. How did the lecture go?' the familiar voice of Sukhbir asked.

'I had an inkling it might be you, old friend. The lecture went well, thank you.' Barun said. 'And how are you doing?'

'Fine. I'm doing fine.' There was little emotion in Sukbir's voice. 'I've just come off the phone to an old acquaintance of ours. Do you recall the possession case we had in Tower Hamlets some years ago?'

Memories of that day came flooding back to Barun. 'There's hardly a chance that I will ever forget that experience.' From time to time, he still heard those shrieks in his dreams.

'You are not alone there.' Sukhbir paused before going on. 'Well, the constable we met that day was called Jenny, and she has phoned me completely out of the blue. There's this small village called Corvid's Head where she is based these days.'

The name rang a bell with Barun. 'That's an island, isn't it?

'That's right. You might've seen it mentioned in a few of the newspapers in the past week,' Sukhbir said. 'Ms. Jones is an inspector now and called me because they've been having some problems.'

Barun's eyebrows drew together. 'What kind of problems?'

*

Dipping and raising, the road snaked across the landscape; Soumili wondered to herself if they would have reached the house by now if the roads on the island had been built straighter. They passed by lush pastures where sleepy cattle were grazing in the heat of the mid-afternoon sun.

'By the way, we're getting rid of that horrid cabinet as soon as possible,' she said, winding the passenger window down further.

Her husband turned and gave her a playful smile. 'You haven't even properly looked at it yet, dear.'

'I saw enough of the ugly thing in one of the auctioneer's pictures, though.' Soumili wrinkled her nose. 'We'll have to see if there is a charity shop nearby that will take it off our hands.'

Harmesh laughed. 'Let's just put off making any plans shall we. Anyway, we should be counting our blessings: there aren't many properties that come fully furnished. Imagine if we had had to buy everything new?'

'In some ways, I might've preferred that,' Soumili said. 'It feels a bit strange taking all of a dead woman's belongings.'

Clicking his tongue, Harmesh rolled his eyes. 'She's not dead. The auctioneer told me that she'd just gone to live in a care home. Besides, her son has apparently already taken away most of her keepsakes so all we have is the furniture.' He took one hand off the steering wheel to pat her on the back. 'Don't be stressing yourself with such trivial matters. We've barely been married two weeks; you're supposed to be all calm and relaxed.'

Soumili put her hand over her shoulder and caressed his fingers. 'I know. I just want everything to be. . . perfect.'

'And it will be,' he said, returning his hand to the wheel. 'I promise.'

Eventually, they drove over a brow of a hill and caught sight of their new home for the first time. Neither of them spoke to one another as they stared in amazement at the house. The pictures had not done it justice. For a building that was hundreds of years old, it was in a remarkable condition, and the window frames and doors had been freshly painted since the photographs had been taken.

'It's huge!' Soumili exclaimed.

Harmesh gave a shrug. 'Plenty of room for children.'

As arranged, an employee of the auctioneers was waiting in the front garden for them. After they had parked up, they gave her a wave and approached her.

'You must be Susan. We spoke the other day,' Soumili said, shaking her hand.

Soumili was expecting the cheery lady who she had spoken with over the phone, but Susan appeared rather dazed, her face ashen.

'Oh, yes. . . pleased to meet you.' The woman cast a glance to one of the upstairs windows.

'Are you okay?' Harmesh asked, lowering his head to draw eye level with the woman.

After staring blankly at him for a couple of seconds, Susan's body jerked. 'Sorry, the last five minutes have been rather peculiar, and I'm still a bit flummoxed in all honesty.

I thought you'd beaten me here because I saw somebody in the window.' She pointed upwards. 'When I got in though I realised straight away that I must've been mistaken. You see, the door to that bedroom was locked when I tried to get in. You must think I'm rather silly bringing up such nonsense.'

'Not at all. Your mind can play tricks on you of course.' Harmesh gave a warm smile. 'Though are you sure that there isn't an intruder in the house?'

Susan fervently shook her head. 'Oh no, that's not a possibility. If there really had been anyone in the room, they would've had to have passed me to make their escape, and I also went as far checking all the other rooms. I even looked under the beds and in the closets. On top of that, like I said, the door was locked.'

'Let's just draw a line under all this.' Soumili raised her hands. 'I'm quite tired and would like a sit down.'

Susan's mood brightened. 'Of course. I'll let you inside,' she said, rummaging around in her handbag for a set of keys.

The living room was the epitome of rustic, a musty smell to the air. No matter how hard she tried to examine the individual features of the room, Soumili's attention was always drawn to the fireplace. It was certainly imposing, the firebox so deep that it was big enough for two people to fit inside it providing they were crouching down.

'The son of the former owner told me that you'll never get any draughts coming from there in the winter months,' Susan said after noticing Soumili's gaze.

'It's all wonderful.' Harmesh scanned the room. 'What word am I looking for? Authentic? No, homely! That's it!'

Soumili did not entirely agree with her husband, but she did not voice her opinion. 'Where does that door lead to?' she asked, pointing to an unassuming door.

'Ah yes, the basement.' Susan rolled her eyes whilst smirking. 'As we were talking about over the phone, I think you'll have your work cut out down there. At least it's spacious anyway.'

Opening the door, Soumili saw immediately what the woman meant. There were thick layers of dust on cardboard boxes that were pushed up against one of the walls, whilst the floorboards were in a state of disrepair. She ventured down the steps with Harmesh leaving Susan in the living room.

'Plenty of potential,' Harmesh said optimistically. 'We could convert it into a games room or perhaps even a children's play area.'

'Maybe after you've vacuumed the place several hundred times.' She gave him a playful jab in the ribs. Out of the corner of her eye, Soumili perceived that one of the floorboards was dislodged. 'And you also might want to fetch a hammer to nail that plank back down.'

Harmesh wrapped his arms around her. 'All in good time, my dear.'

After they had finished embracing, they began to walk hand in hand up the steps, but Soumili stopped and pulled away. There was something poking out from under the displaced board. Wandering over to it, she bent down and discovered that it was a book.

'What've you got there?' Harmseh asked.

She picked the book up and ran her fingers over its leather cover. Peculiar painted stones were embedded into the cover, and Soumili realised that unlike everything else in the basement, the book was free of dust.

'I do apologise, but I'm going to have to leave now to make my other appointment,' Susan called down the stairs.

'We'll be right up,' Harmesh replied. 'Are you coming, Soumili?'

She had been on the verge of opening the book, but following the interruption, Soumili chose instead to carefully place it down on one of the boxes before following her husband up the steps.

Susan pulled open the front door then handed over the keys. 'Well then, there you go.'

'Many thanks for all your help, Susan.' Harmesh smiled. 'Before you leave, there is one thing that has been nagging me: why was the house up for auction rather than for sale through an estate agent?'

Susan shrugged. 'Some people just want to sell properties as quickly as they can; I guess the former owner's family just wanted someone to come along to take it off their hands pronto. From your perspective, you would have probably spent thousands more if it hadn't come through an auctioneer like us.'

'Lucky us,' Harmesh said, looking at the ceiling.

'Sorry, I better be off. My number is on the table if you need anything.' Susan gave a timid wave.

'Safe travels,' Soumili said as the woman departed.

Alone in their new house for the first time, Soumili and Harmesh made for the kitchen to boil the kettle. Some basic provisions had been left behind, and thankfully a tin of teabags was amongst them.

'Why were you bothered about how the house was sold?' Soumili asked.

'Don't you find it odd as well? A smaller house down the road from here was listed at nearly twice the price. By all accounts, we shouldn't have been able to afford a place like this,' he said as he poured a drink.

'Like you said before, lucky us.' Soumili raised her eyebrows.

'I suppose so,' Harmesh said, handing her a drink. 'Right, I'm just going to get our suitcases from the car. You take the weight off your feet, dear.'

He kissed her on the forehead then left the house. Taking a seat at the kitchen table, Soumili placed both her hands around her mug and watched as the steam rose from the drink. All of a sudden, an urge came over her to cast her gaze to the small window that was directly behind her.

When she turned around, she found on the other side of the pane nothing but a dried leaf caught in a cobweb.

The second she looked away, however, she felt the urge once again. This time she got to her feet and strode to the window to look out at the garden. A row of ash trees could be seen beyond the thorny hedge that rang along the garden wall, whilst the back gate had a padlock on its latch.

Soumili could not see a single living creature. Shaking her head to herself, she drew the curtain. The strange thing was that now she could no longer see out of one window, Soumili felt a compulsion to look out of another.

*

The sound of the ship's horn awoke Barun. The effects of having not slept in a proper bed for two nights were beginning to take a toll on his body, particularly on his back. Lying on a bench in one of the ship's hallways, his pillow and blanket for the night journey had been his suitcase and his coat respectively. Yesterday he had been given a choice: wait a day for the next commercial ferry or travel to the island that very evening on a cargo ship. He opted for the latter. The ship's captain, a burly war veteran who was proudly wearing on his chest an assortment of medals, appeared and headed towards him.

'Afraid it's hardly fine cuisine, squire,' the captain said, handing him a mess tin.

Barun studied the contents of the tin and put on a brave face. 'Thank you, captain. Are we nearly at Corvid's Head?'

'That we are, squire,' the captain replied. 'Bit of fog on the waters so we've slowed our approach a tad.'

After the captain went on his way, Barun stretched his shoulders. He could only stomach a few mouthfuls of his tepid porridge, discarding the rest in a dustbin as he made his way to the deck.

The sea breeze was the perfect tonic to his drowsy state. It was not long before the ship passed through the mist and the shores of Corvid's Head came into view. The island was much bigger than Barun had anticipated, and the sheer cliff faces that made up most of its coastline were as beautiful as they were formidable. Barun could immediately infer from Sukhbir's rested eyes and clean hair that he had been fortunate enough to catch an earlier ferry, and had therefore reached the island before him with time to recuperate from the choppy journey. Sukhbir was waiting for him on the waterfront when the ship moved into dock.

Making his way down the gangway, Barun hailed his colleague. 'Good morning.'

'Ahoy, my friend,' Sukhbir said. 'How are you?'

'A little tired but fine otherwise. And you?'

'I am okay.' Sukhbir gestured inland. 'I've rented a car, but I'm afraid that I wasn't able to park very close to the dock.'

'That's alright, I could do with stretching my legs,' he said as they started walking. 'Have there been any developments since we last spoke?'

'Not as such. I spoke to Inspector Jones late last night, but she had nothing new to report,'

Sukhbir said. 'I'm already underway with my research and collated a few newspaper articles of interest from the local library.'

'Very good.' Barun nodded. 'Have you spoken to any of the locals?'

Sukhbir scanned the area to see if anyone was within earshot of them. 'Look, Barun, obviously I've not met many of the people here, though from what I have seen so far they don't appear to be the friendliest of folk. They're set in their ways and distrustful of outsiders. Whatever you do, don't tell them what you do for a living.'

'Duly noted,' Barun said, taking a cigar from the inside pocket of his coat.

The inspector had told Sukhbir that she was having a meeting at the town hall that morning, and so he dropped Barun at the building before driving off to continue with his research. As Barun was walking up the steps, he was approached by a middle-aged man with a notepad in his hand.

'Mister Rai?' the stranger asked.

Barun stopped but not before he had put a fair distance between himself and the man. 'That is me.'

'I work for the Corvid Chronicle. Is it true that you are some sort of investigator of ghosts?'

How the heck did he know that I would be here? Barun thought to himself. 'I am a private investigator.'

'And you're here to look into the recent spate of suicides, yes?' the journalist asked, his lip twisting into a wry smile.

'Unfortunately, I am not at liberty to say anymore. Good day to you.' Barun marched away from the man before he could question him further.

The meeting had just concluded when he entered into the hall, a grand room that was let down somewhat by its threadbare curtains. It was fortunate that Inspector Jones was wearing her uniform as Barun may not have recognised her otherwise. They exchanged a subtle nod with one another from opposite sides of the room. Once the throng of people had thinned out, she approached him.

'Barun, good to see you again,' she said. 'I wish we were meeting under better circumstances.'

'Yes, I get that a lot.' Barun saw out of the corner of his eye that two men that had been in deep conversation nearby had stopped talking, and they were now watching him attentively. 'Perhaps there is somewhere more private we can speak.'

They found an empty office which appeared as though it was seldom used, a grubby mop propped up against the desk.

'Thank you for coming so quickly, Barun.' Jenny moved to look out of the window. 'I'm guessing Sukhbir has already filled you in?'

'He has told me the basics,' Barun said.

'Good.' Jenny nodded. 'Before I forget, I should warn you that word has got out about your arrival, so you may receive some unwanted attention. How the newspapers figured out you were coming in such a short space of time is beyond me.'

'I have actually already run into one of the local journalists.' Barun perched himself on the desk. 'I don't anticipate that they will hinder my work too much. Often

I find that there is initially a bit of a furore when I begin an investigation before the press gets bored with me and moves on to a new story.'

Jenny turned to him. 'Another matter that I wish to discuss is a sensitive one. Sukhbir said to me that you have research grants that will cover the cost of your expenses, though I don't feel comfortable with you receiving nothing for your trouble. It is my intention to ask my superiors–.'

Barun held up a hand. 'It is most kind of you to consider this, but Sukhbir and I are not in need of money, nor are we motivated by it. If you don't mind, I would like to talk about the case.'

'Very well. Maybe I can buy you a bottle of wine or something instead.' Jenny's face then darkened. 'This morning I had a discussion with the pathologist who had examined the body. His report was both strange and disturbing. Petechiae, marks normally present on victims of asphyxiation, were around the dead man's eyes.'

'Yet Sukhbir told me that there was no one close to him when he jumped,' he said, bemusement in his tone of voice.

'That is correct, and I have the pictures to prove it.' Jenny pursed her lips briefly as her eyes gradually glazed over. 'Photographs can, on occasion, capture the unexplainable. Those that were taken in the final moments of that man's life are. . . astonishing. They reminded me almost instantly of our experience with that young woman all those years ago, which was the last time I could not fathom something that was right in front of me. Well, I have had copies made of these pictures so you will see for yourself.'

'And who took these photos?' Barun asked.

Jenny snapped out of her dreamy state. 'Just the local oddball. We are, however, monitoring him as this is not the first time he has been found lurking in those parts with his camera. He's harmless, I'm sure of that, yet there's something that I can't put my finger on.'

'It sounds like it might be an idea for me to speak with this young fellow at some stage,' Barun said. 'For now, though, I wish to visit the site.'

'I can drive you over now if you like?' Jenny suggested.

'Actually, I was thinking of walking there. It would be beneficial for me to experience the island; you know, ambling along its paths and breathing its air.'

Jenny frowned. 'If you wish, though, I must say that it is a fair walk.'

The inspector had not exaggerated. It took Barun a few minutes shy of half an hour to reach the cliffs. The route, however, had been simple enough as he was able to remain on the same stretch of pavement for most of his journey. He may have spent a while searching for the exact area of the cliffs where the tragedy had unfolded if Jenny had not told him to bear right once he came across an uprooted tree. Wandering over to the cliff edge, Barun peeked down at the crashing waves below. He did not linger there for long as standing mere feet away from certain death started to make him feel queasy. Dropping to one knee, he pushed his palm into the grass and focused his mind. There was nothing. All that could be heard was the lapping of the waves below.

Puzzled by his failure to connect with the spirit world, he tightly closed his eyes and poured all his energy into trying to establish a link. Yet again, there was nothing. Even in places that had seen little in way of death, Barun was still able to make out faint echoes of distant spirits. For an individual with Barun's gifts to neither see or hear anything from the other side whilst stood upon a cliff where so many had died was something that should have been impossible. He scanned his surroundings for whatever was blocking his visions, though he was not sure what he was looking for.

Despite the history of the cliffs, it was a placid place with only a few hard features here and there, such as an ugly tree half-hanging over the edge. Barun decided that there was no reason for him to spend any more time at the cliffs, and he turned to head back the way he had came.

As he ambled back to the village, he set eyes on a house that he had not noticed before. It was an impressive red brick building set amongst woodland. By chance, a dog walker was passing by, and Barun hailed them.

'I am sorry to bother, but do you happen to know anything about that house?'

Not looking to the house, the woman tightened her grip on the leash. 'That place? They call that the House on the Cliff. A friend of my mother's used to live there until quite recently. Think it's been bought by some young couple.'

'Must have cost them a fortune.' Barun placed his hands in his pockets.

'I wouldn't know. Good day,' she abruptly said before resuming her stroll.

Barun stood still for a while, studying the house. Shaking his head to himself, he once more began to walk in the direction of the village.

CHAPTER FOUR

In the cupboard under the sink, Harmesh found a bottle of scotch. It was certainly not the drink Soumili would have chosen as a toast to their new home, but by the time they had unfinished unpacking, neither of them had the energy to travel to a shop. They had a relaxed afternoon together, listening to the radio whilst dozing upon the sofa. Soumili was wary that she was to start her new job in the morning, and for this reason she left most of the bottle to her husband. She was half-asleep and resting her head on Harmesh's chest when he suddenly leapt to his feet.

'What is it?' she asked in a panic.

He gave no reply, storming over to the front door and throwing it open. Pursuing her husband, Soumili found him in the garden confronting a stranger.

'What do you think you are doing?' Harmesh demanded, his hands clutching the stranger's shirt collar.

Wearing a grey ushanka hat, the young man had a camera around his neck, and his expression clearly showed that he was deeply distressed from being manhandled.

'I was just. . . the curtain was open,' the young man spluttered.

Harmesh scowled. 'What's your damn name?'

'B-Brian.'

Gradually, Harmesh's face softened. 'If I ever catch you around here again, Brian, I'll phone the police. Do you understand?'

Brian furiously nodded. Relinquishing his hold of the intruder, Harmesh grabbed his camera from him and opened its compartment. He pulled out its roll of film then handed the camera back to him.

'I'm keeping this,' Harmesh said, holding the negatives up between his thumb and forefinger. 'Get out of my sight.'

Brian did not need to be told twice, and he scampered off into the night.

'Are you okay, Harmesh?' Soumili asked in a quiet voice from the doorstep.

'Fine.' He watched the young man until he was out of sight before walking back into the house. Once they were both back inside, Harmesh strode round the house with great purpose shutting every curtain. Once he had pulled the back door's bolt across, he poured himself another drink.

Soumili sat down. 'Shouldn't we phone the police?'

'He was just some kooky kid. I think I gave him a good scare so I doubt he'll be back anytime soon.' He took a sip of his drink.

Taking a look at her watch, Soumili let out a gasp. 'Have you seen the time? There is no way that I will be able to get a good night's sleep after all this commotion.'

Harmesh was once more raising his glass to his lips, but he stopped then placed it down on a coffee table. 'Wipe the whole thing from your mind, my dear. It's all over now, so let's just get to bed. I'm sure you'll fall asleep as soon as your head hits the pillow.'

He was wrong. Tossing and turning in their bed, Soumili was still wide awake several hours later. Eventually, she turned her alarm clock to face away from her so that she could no longer see how late it was. Whilst she was repositioning herself for the umpteenth time, there came a clang from downstairs. It was by no means a tremendous noise, Harmesh not even stirring in his slumber, though it did reverberate for a couple of seconds. She prodded him in the arm. 'Harmesh.'

Grunting, he rolled to his other side. Soumili contemplated trying again to wake him; however, she decided to investigate alone, partly because she knew how hard it was to awaken Harmesh after he had had a couple of drinks, but also because she was confident that there was no intruder in the house. Despite her confidence, she armed herself with a hefty vase from the windowsill. Soumili left the room and crept down the stairs, the antique floorboards groaning with every step she took. Her breath caught in her throat when she reached the bottom to find that the light in the kitchen was on, though Soumili's shock soon evaporated when she remembered that she had forgotten to flick the switch before she had retired to bed. On the kitchen floor there lay the cause of the disturbance: a stainless steel ladle.

Smiling to herself, she picked it up and returned it to its stand. She was on the verge of returning to her bedroom when the very same compulsion that she had had that afternoon came over her. Switching off the light switch, she shuffled towards the window. Initially hesitating, Soumili pulled back the curtain partway. Moonlight bathed the garden. Just as before, the gate was shut and nothing at all seemed amiss. Soumili leaned her face closer to the pane. A pale hand sprang up from below, its palm hitting the outside of the window with a dull thud. Petrified, she recoiled back and watched the hand as it dragged its nails vertically across the glass. She blinked. The hand was nowhere to be seen. Gasping for air, Soumili grabbed onto a chair to prevent herself from crumpling to the ground. After what felt like hours, she gathered the courage to surge at the window to draw its curtain.

*

Newspaper clippings upon his chest, Barun awoke with his glasses still on his face. He had inadvertently spent the night upon a sofa with his feet dangling over one of its arms. Above him he could hear Sukhbir pacing back and forth in his own room whilst speaking to someone over the phone. Barun collected the articles into a bundle and sat up. The headline of the clipping at the top of the pile caught his attention: Two Tragedies in Two Weeks. It was dated 2nd September 1959 and included a grainy photograph of the cliff edge. Just as he began to read the body of the article, there came a knock at the door and Sukhbir entered.

'I didn't rent this cottage for you to spend the night on a sofa.' Sukhbir grinned.

'It is remarkably comfortable, I must say.' Barun started to light up. 'Who were you talking to?'

'It was Jenny. She received a call this morning regarding a bizarre disturbance at some old house. The reason she was ringing was because she reckons it might be of interest to us.'

Barun took the lit cigar from his mouth. 'By any chance, are we talking about the House on the Cliff?'

'How the heck did you know that?' Sukhbir asked, giving him a quizzical look.

'Intuition.' With a mischievous smile, Barun tapped his temple with his forefinger.

After Barun had changed his shirt and splashed some water on his face, they drove to the house. Jenny had arrived before them, and she was stood by her car speaking with a broad- shouldered sergeant.

'Inspector, good morning,' Barun said as he and Sukhbir walked towards the police car.

'Ah, morning to you both.' She smiled. 'This is Sergeant Stepney. We have just been talking about you.'

The sergeant stared askance at the men. 'Morning, lads,' he said in a dour voice.

'I'm breaking a couple of protocols in inviting private investigators to a call-out, but when I spoke to residents this morning I felt I had no other option. It won't have escaped your attention that this is the closest building to where the man died.' Jenny gave a vague wave towards the cliff edge. 'Now, there's no suggestion yet that last night's disturbance is directly linked to the death, though I have this inkling that we might be able to shed some light on that affair if we can find out what happened here.'

'We'll try not to get under your feet,' Barun said.

The four headed along the garden path and rang the doorbell. A man with a sturdy frame and square jaw answered the door. 'Thank you for coming.' He stood aside for them to enter into his home.

'You must be Harmesh,' Jenny said. 'I am Inspector Jones and this is Sergeant Stepney. With us we also have Barun and Sukhbir who are private investigators.'

Harmesh nodded. 'Nice to meet you all. Soumili is in the kitchen.'

Her black, wavy hair tied back into a plait, a lady wearing the uniform of a nurse was sat at the table. 'I'm very appreciative that you've come out to see us so quickly. Sorry that I can't offer you all a seat.'

'No problem at all,' Barun said. 'My associate and I have no issue standing.'

The rest of them seated themselves at the table, Jenny positioning herself opposite to the homeowners.

'It is probably best you start from the top,' Jenny said in a reassuring tone.

'Course.' Soumili took a deep breath. 'During the night I heard a noise and came downstairs to check it out. Found a ladle on the floor over there and put it back in its place. Naturally, I thought myself rather silly at getting worked up over a utensil and started to make my way back to bed.

Then, I can't explain why, but I felt the need to look outside. Nothing at first caught my eye and then.. . then. . . ' Soumili trailed off, biting her bottom lip. 'This grotesque hand appeared and hit the window. They must have been crouching down waiting for me.'

Harmesh took a hold of his wife's hand then looked to the inspector. 'What kind of sick mind would do such a thing?' he asked.

'A wrong'un, that's who,' the sergeant chipped in.

'Did you catch sight of the person's face? Or did this hand have any distinctive features?' Jenny asked Soumili.

The woman gave a despondent shake of her head.

'I reckon I know who it is.' Harmesh folded his arms. 'Last night I caught a young man stood outside our living room window taking pictures of us. I warned him that I'd contact the authorities if I ever found him on our property again, so I certainly have no qualms about telling you that his name was Brian, or so he claimed.'

Jenny and the sergeant exchanged a glance.

'And I have already told you, Harmesh, that it was not him.' Soumili sighed.

'Why are you so sure of that?' Jenny asked.

'Because the arm was too thin. . . I would go as far as describing it as almost emaciated.' Soumili checked her watch. 'I'm very sorry, I'm going to have to leave. I was supposed to start my new job at the hospital this morning, but I had to phone in to let them know I was going to be late.'

'That's fine,' Jenny said. 'I think we probably have everything we need. Gentlemen, is there anything you want to bring up or ask?'

'There is one thing: if that ladle had not fallen, you would not have gone downstairs.' Barun narrowed his eyes in thought.

'What's your point?' the sergeant asked brusquely.

'My point is that if it was some practical joker standing outside, you were actually drawn from your bedroom by something out of their control. Soumili, are you positive that there wasn't anyone other than you and Harmesh in the house?' Barun asked.

Soumili looked down at the table. 'As it happens, the thought did cross my mind, but there were no signs of a break-in.'

'Yes, I think it's quite clear that there was no forced entry.' Sergeant Stepney pushed his chair back abruptly. 'Thank you for bringing this all to our attention. We best let you get on with your day.'

All those that were seated rose from their chairs. Walking in single file, they were shown out of the house. Sukhbir stopped suddenly on the doorstep and bent down to collect something from the ground.

'Is this yours?' he asked Harmesh, lifting up a book.

Harmesh gave a bemused twist of his lip. 'No, it's not ours. Soumili found it in the basement the other day, but I have no idea how it ended up out here.'

Sukhbir began to flick through its pages. 'Do you mind if I borrow it?'

'Borrow it? You can have it if you want.' Harmesh gave a dismissive wave.

'If you have any further issues with trespassers or anything else, please do not hesitate to contact us again.' Jenny gave a smile and a nod to Harmesh and Soumili.

'Thank you, inspector. Take care now,' Soumili said.

The police officers and the investigators headed in silence to their cars, Sukhbir continuing to peruse through the book as he walked. When they arrived, Jenny turned and raised her eyebrows at the others.

'That was interesting, but perhaps not in the way I was expecting,' she said.

'Aye, we know that young Brian is an even bigger menace than we once thought.' Sergeant Stepney scratched at some stubble on his chin. 'Me and one of the constables will pick him up later.'

'What about this mystery hand? Do either of you have any thoughts on that?' Barun asked the officers.

'Maybe Brian's found himself an accomplice of sorts,' Jenny suggested.

'Or, more likely, the woman was seeing things.' The sergeant looked back to the house.

'After all, it was late at night, and she was clearly put out about what had happened earlier in the evening.'

'Do you two gentlemen have any theories?' Jenny asked.

Although she was addressing both of the investigators, Sukhbir was so engrossed in the book that he did not look up.

'I have many,' Barun said, 'but theories are cheap. I need a lot more evidence before I dare speak any of my ideas aloud. Now, before we go our separate ways, I would like to request the contact details of a relative of the deceased.'

'That would be his fiancée.' Stepney clenched his jaw. 'We've already spoken with her, and she has nothing more to say.'

'With all due respect, I think my line of questioning will be very different to that of a police officer,' Barun said.

Drawing up to his full height, it appeared for a moment that Sergeant Stepney was about to launch into a tirade. Jenny stared ferociously at him, and the sergeant's expression softened.

'My sergeant makes a good point. Adrian Worthington's fiancée has already been interviewed, and furthermore, she remains utterly distraught about his death,' Jenny said. 'If you genuinely believe, however, that speaking to her may help, I will give you her phone number. There is one condition: should she say that she does not want to speak with you, end the call and do not phone her again.'

'Of course.' Barun nodded. 'I would not dream of pestering a person in grief.'

As Jenny jotted down the telephone number, a great cloud above them parted which revealed the sun. In the blink of an eye, the island became greener, more vibrant. The intensity of the glare, however, was so strong that Barun felt compelled to reach into his pocket and he produced his sunglasses.

'There.' Jenny handed him the piece of paper. 'Tell her that you got the number from me.'

'Thank you,' Barun said. 'No doubt we will see each other again soon.'

Barun and Sukhbir left the company of the police officers and got into their rented car.

'I can tell by the expression on your face that what you have there is something remarkable.'

Barun gestured towards the book.

'Remarkable? It is far more than that, my friend.' Sukhbir's eyes were wild whilst one of his knees was trembling ever-so-slightly. 'To think we just found it in someone's front garden.'

Barun had never seen the man in such a childlike awe, and he subtly plucked the book from his grasp. Straightway, Barun could see why Sukhbir was so amazed. He was by no means proficient in ancient languages; however, he could identify at least two of the writing systems.

'Unless I'm mistaken, that there is Sumerian.' Barun ran his finger down the page.

'Yes. By my reckoning it's Classical Sumerian,' Sukhbir said. 'The writer also uses Aramaic and Hittite along with several other languages that I cannot put my finger on quite yet. Whoever composed this work was certainly a master scholar in early languages.'

'How old do you think this is?' Barun asked, carefully turning another page.

'Although it is rather tattered in places, the yellowing would suggest that it's not that old in the grand scheme of things. My rough estimate is that it could be between forty and seventy years old.' Sukhbir started the ignition. 'The appearance of such a peculiar thing raises an obvious question: is this connected with our case? Thankfully, I always travel with one or two books on ancient writing systems.'

Barun laughed. 'You know, when most people go travelling, they tend to fill their suitcases with things like sandals and Hawaiian shirts.'

'Luckily for us, I'm not most people.' Sukhbir gave a wry smile. 'Anyway, hopefully I'll be able to find an answer to your question soon enough.'

Raising an eyebrow, Barun inclined his head towards his friend. 'That'll take you hours.'

'Well, at the moment we've get precious few other leads.' Sukhbir put the car into gear, and they pulled away. 'Unless you have had any conveniently-timed visions which may relate to the case, that is.'

Barun cleared his throat. 'I haven't seen or heard a single spirit since I set foot on the island.'

The car decelerated a little. 'What? How is that possible?' Sukhbir asked.

'I have already asked myself that several times. Powerful spirits have in the past hindered my ability, but this is something different,' Barun said. 'I had delayed revealing this to you as part of me was hoping that it was just some blip. Unfortunately, I now know for sure that there is a phantom upon this island, and it is capable of blocking my capacity to observe the spirit realm. Whatever this malevolence is, it does not want to be found.'

'That's indeed disturbing. Well, if we cannot depend on your visions, then we'll have to rely on more traditional methods of investigation. I would quite like to go door to door asking folk if they've seen anything unexplainable, but I doubt Inspector Jones would be all too happy about that.'

Barun looked out of his window towards the sea. 'I don't think that that would be a worthwhile exercise anyway. These people may have encountered this spectre on many occasions for all we know, yet they are scared. In fact, I would go as far as saying that they are petrified. I have seen it in their eyes. They cannot comprehend this terror that is lurking just outside of their line of sight, and so they bury their heads in the sand, pretending that it is nothing but their imaginations. No, I am afraid that there are precious few people here that are open-minded enough to acknowledge what they have witnessed.'

'So you are saying that they refuse to believe their own eyes?' Sukhbir asked.

'Yes,' Barun replied. 'And who can blame them? When it comes to distressing matters it is practically always easier to ignore the truth than it is to accept it.'

*

There came the unmistakable creak of the letterbox followed by the sound of something light dropping into the cage below. Placing the novel he had been reading down on the arm of his chair, Father Paul pulled himself to his feet and walked from his cosy living room to his front door. A piece of folded, violet-coloured cardboard was sat at the bottom of the letter cage. He pulled back the net curtain of the nearby window to see who it was that had posted the message, but the person was now out of sight. Lifting the lid of the cage, he picked up the note and unfolded it. The ink was rather faint, and Father Paul positioned his reading glasses further down his nose to help him make out the words. It read in block capitals: SHE HAS LEFT THE HOUSE AND NEWCOMERS HAVE MOVED IN.

He stood in contemplation, idly tearing the card into four segments. It was news that he had been expecting for some months. Leaving his cottage, he cycled to the church where he found his mentor, Father Damon, sat on the front pew.

'I wasn't expecting to see you today, Father,' the old priest said without turning his head.

'Has an urgent matter arisen?'

'In all honesty, Father, I do not know.' Father Paul sat down next to him. 'A note has just now come through my door saying that Agatha is no longer living at the House on the Cliff.' Father Damon rubbed his palm against the handle of his walking stick. 'Do you know who sent you this note?'

'Presumably a concerned congregant of ours, though their identity I do not know,' Father

Pail said, staring ahead at the altar.

'So there are people other than us that are troubled about that place.' The old man gave a sigh. 'I warned that son of hers that we must be contacted long before any new owners moved in. We can only hope that we are being irrational fools, and that there is nothing to fear in that house.'

'What of Father Edward's account? Is that not evidence enough that the house is unsafe?' Father Paul asked.

'That was twenty years ago, my friend. He was as old as I am now when he told me of his experiences there. Perhaps his ageing eyes were deceived that day. Then again, we cannot take that risk.'

Father Paul turned his head. 'What do you propose?'

'I will go there and bless the house. If the blessing is uneventful, we can presume that all is well,' the old priest said.

Screwing his face up into an incredulous expression, Father Paul shook his head. 'No, I won't let you do that. If any of us are to venture to that place, it should be me.'

The old priest raised one of his wild, grey eyebrows. 'I cannot say that I am altogether happy with that notion.'

'I do not intend to offend you when I say that my decision is final.' Father Paul got to his feet.

'Yes, I may be in my twilight years, yet I am still perceptive enough to see that much,' the old priest said. 'Heed this warning: do not linger in that house. Once the blessing is finished, then you must immediately leave. Understood?'

'Understood.'

Father Paul approached the altar then crossed himself. For a moment, he stayed there as though waiting for something to happen before he headed down the aisle. Collecting the necessary paraphernalia, the priest mounted his bike and set off for the House on the Cliff. Normally he would have enjoyed a long ride in pleasant weather, but his anxiety had manifested as a churning sensation in his stomach. This sense of dread subsided slightly when he caught sight of the house; he had always found its exterior to hold an endearing quaintness. He propped his bike against a wall and, after taking a deep breath, rang the doorbell. By the time the door was opened, Father Paul was beginning to wonder whether he should come back another day.

A young woman with big eyes answered the door. 'Hello?'

'Good afternoon. My name is Father Paul.'

'Oh, hello. I'm Soumili,' she said. 'Would you like to come in?'

'Thank you.' Father Paul stepped over the threshold. 'On behalf of everyone on the island, I would like to welcome you to our little community.'

'I greatly appreciate that.' She gave the hint of a smile. 'Sorry I took so long to come to the door; my husband and I were having a drink in the garden as I've just finished my first day at my new job.'

'No problem at all.' Father Paul grinned. 'And if I may inquire, where is it that you work?'

'I'm a nurse at the hospital,' she replied.

'A most rewarding job,' he said. 'I must say that I have not just come here to greet you. When people move to the island, I also like to offer to bless their new homes. Would you have any objection to—'

'Of course not,' she cut in. 'Once you're done, if you come through the house to the back garden you can have a drink with my husband and I.'

'That would be lovely.' He gave a nod. 'It won't take long.'

The woman departed leaving Father Paul alone in the living room. After placing his coat upon the handrail of the staircase, he opened his bag. First collecting his cross, he gave it a soft kiss before then picking out his vial of holy water. He began the blessing by sprinkling the water onto the floor.

'O, holy Father, we welcome you into this place. . . '

There came a noise from the fireplace. At first he thought it to simply be the wind whistling through it, but the sound was too intermittent. Cautiously, he approached, and when he came within a few feet of the hearth, a small amount of debris fell down onto the logs. The sound was still present. In fact, it was growing ever louder. It sounded almost like gas escaping from a stove, except there were qualities to it that were close to animalistic. In this dreadful hissing he perceived several emotions, the most clear of which were anger and hate. Taking two more steps, he ducked his head down and peered up the chimney. There was nothing there but a square of daylight thirty feet above. Father Paul, feeling rather foolish, then returned to the middle of the room. For several seconds, there was complete silence, but then he started to make something out. From the fireplace he could hear a scratching that quickly developed into a scurrying noise.

A dark cloud burst from the chimney. Father Paul's cross slipped from his fingers, as he became enveloped in hundreds upon hundreds of insects. So startled was the priest that he did not flail his arms at first. The creatures were as dark as night and unlike any insect that he had ever seen before. Their legs felt like needles upon his skin, and they had tiny teeth which they chattered.

Swept from his feet, an invisible force then dragged him by the ankles towards the fireplace. He desperately clawed at the rug, but it was too powerful for him to oppose. All of a sudden, just before the soles of his shoes had reached the stove, whatever had hold of him released its grip, and the insects then started to dissipate.

'Leave,' a fell voice from the darkness said.

Springing to his feet, Father Paul seized his bag then fled from the house. Even as he mounted his bicycle, he still could not comprehend what had just occurred. Had it been his imagination? No, it cannot have been that, as his face was stinging from where the beasts had scratched at him. The ride back to the church was a blur to him; on more than one occasion he had almost ridden out into oncoming traffic. Before he entered the church he took a deep breath whilst wiping the sweat from his brow with a handkerchief. Walking into the nave, he found his mentor stood staring at the altar. He could tell by Father Damon's rigid stance that the old man had grown tense during his wait.

'Tell me,' he demanded without turning to face his peer.

'I have failed,' Father Paul said in a feeble voice.

'Failed, failed, failed,' his mentor grumbled, almost to himself. 'We can't afford failure, Father Paul. Helpless lambs. . . ' He started to idly wander around. 'We can't do anything against such a powerful spirit, and it's necessary to recognise our limitations. The best way we can serve our flock is to steer them away from the danger.'

'I do not think we can simply ignore this,' Father Paul said.

'And what would you do, my friend? Contact the bishop? He could not even be bothered to give us advice when our roof was damaged last year. No, I know of no one who can help us.' The veteran priest gave a sullen shrug. 'Vigilance is our only weapon against this foe.'

Father Paul knew well that it was impossible to change his mentor's mind when he was in this sort of mood. Then again, the more he thought about it, the old man was right. What could they do?

CHAPTER FIVE

The phone was answered on the fourth ring. There came a scratching noise as the person who had picked up the receiver fumbled at it.

'Hello?' a hoarse yet timid voice answered.

'Is this Michelle Worthington?' Barun asked in a soft tone.

'Speaking,' she replied.

'My name is Barun Rai, and your number was given to me by Inspector Jones.'

There was a prolonged period of silence. 'This is about Adrian, isn't it?' she eventually asked. 'I have already told the police all I know.'

'I appreciate that you have already spoken with them, but I would like to ask questions that they are unlikely to have asked,' Barun said. 'It should not take long, I promise.'

'Fine,' Michelle said curtly. 'Just get on with it, yeah? I've just about had enough of telling people the same things over and over again.'

'Thank you. I wanted to first ask if he spoke of anything peculiar in the week leading up to his death?'

'Well, the first thing I noticed was that he went off his food; he barely ate a morsel some days. Then there was the wandering. Adrian always was a night owl, but I'd never known him sneak out of the house in early hours of the morning before. I started to grow suspicious that he might be. .. well. . . ' she trailed off. 'He kept mentioning this woman.'

'Woman?'

'To be honest, I think she was some hallucination or what have you. He swore that he saw her everywhere he went. Two days before his death he even pointed her out to me in the high street, but there was no one there.' She breathed out. 'It became an obsession of his towards the end.'

'And did he ever describe this person?'

'Not all,' she replied. 'I once pressed him about what she looked like, yet he avoided the question. He did talk a little about this book she supposedly gave him though.'

Barun's grip on the receiver tightened. 'What book is this?'

'Oh, it's just some ugly, old thing about wildlife. He wouldn't let me look at it while he was alive. Curiosity got the better of me the other day, and I got it from his trunk. Whatever I had been expecting, it wasn't that. The book is in absolute tatters, and he – I presume it was him – had been using it as a sketchbook of sorts.'

'What was drawn in it?' he asked.

The line went quiet for three seconds.

'I didn't look at it for long. As far as I'm aware, he was never much of an artist which made them even more shocking. I can't put into words the horrible things that are scrawled in it,' she said in a monotonous tone as though she was speaking to herself. 'If it would help you, you can take it off my hands. The police haven't seen it yet.'

'Providing it's not inconvenient to you, I would be most grateful if I could come round to collect it,' he said.

'Okay, but I will leave it on my garden wall: I do not feel up to seeing anyone today.' The woman cleared her throat. 'I live at 3 Parish Way. Goodbye, Mister Rai.'

She ended the call without giving him a chance to say farewell. Immediately, Barun headed up the stairs to Sukhbir's room. He found his associate hunched over a desk, his nose practically touching the book that he was studying.

'Made any headway?' Barun asked.

Puffing out his cheeks, Sukhbir leaned back in his chair. 'I'm getting through it at a snail's pace. So far all I've been able to translate is half a sentence describing the start of some form of ceremony. How did you get on?'

'I believe the deceased did indeed come into contact with a spirit. His fiancée spoke of him becoming obsessed with a woman that no one else could see. As well as that, he was fixated on a certain book.'

Sukhbir raised an eyebrow. 'Not this one here I presume?'

'No, though I must admit that I thought likewise when she first mentioned it.' Barun said.

'I'm going to collect it now once I find a local map.'

'There's one in the magazine stand by the fireplace.' Sukhbir gave a vague gesture. 'By the time you get back I might have finished this sentence.'

After having found the location on the map, Barun set out for the woman's house. The shrill shrieking of gulls filled the afternoon air. Everyone that Barun passed on the footpaths had their heads bowed, and most of them were walking by themselves. Despite getting lost for a brief time, Barun was able to find the home that the late Adrian Worthington had shared with his fiancée.

Partially hidden under a patch of overhanging shrubbery, there was a book with a worn buckram cover upon a brick wall. Barun picked it up. The book had indeed seen better days, and its spine had almost entirely perished; someone had attempted to repair the damage with a thread and needle.

He looked to the house and saw the curtain in the porch stir. Though he was not entirely sure whether the woman was watching him, Barun gave a polite nod before going on his way. Down the road there was a bench by a fountain, and Barun decided that with the weather being agreeable he would sit there to examine the book. Built in the Victorian era, the fountain was both unadorned and modest; however, the water that spouted from it held a remarkable lustre, the falling droplets glistening against the light of the sun. Seating himself, Barun laid the book on his lap and carefully opened it at a random page. Instantly, he understood why the woman had wanted to be rid of it.

Variations of the same subject had been scrawled onto almost every single page. Beady, menacing eyes were staring back at him. It was a woman of sorts, her wild hair floating around her as though she was underwater. Her mouth was agape in a scream, and the veins around her temple were prominent. The man had not written a single word to explain his drawings, whilst the text, that which could be read, offered no hints as to whether the book's subject matter held any relevance.

Eventually, the images became too much even for Barun to bear, and he closed the book. All that could be heard was the gentle swashing from the fountain, and Barun focused on this to help him clear his mind of all the thoughts that were rattling around within his head. Barun was unsure how long he sat peacefully there, but the sky had grown notably darker since he had started his meditations. Though he was confident that the drawings depicted a being that was involved in the man's death, Barun felt no closer to actually identifying her or, more importantly, discovering a way to keep her in check.

*

Though Soumili was mightily puzzled by the priest's sudden disappearance, she did not let it get in the way of her enjoyment of that afternoon. She went out on a peaceful stroll with Harmesh around the cliffs, taking in many beautiful sights along the way. Partway through the walk her husband announced that he wished to wander to the shops before they shut for the evening to pick up a loaf of bread and a few other essentials. Soumili felt drained from her first day at work, and so she opted to return home alone. Her legs were feeling weary by the time she arrived back. Entering her home, she instantly perceived a faint noise coming from the first floor. Throwing her hat and coat down onto a nearby chair, she craned her head to look up the stairs. Soumili sensed something that felt like fingertips brush against her neck, then she yelped as her hair was yanked. To stop herself from going over the bannister, she flung her arms out at the same moment as her hair was released.

Holding her hands close to her chest, she panted whilst scanning her surroundings. She knew this much: there was nothing there on the staircase. With great trepidation, she slowly ascended the steps. Out of the corner of her eye, Soumili thought she saw a movement through the open bedroom door, but when she looked directly inside she quickly realised that there was no one there. This is ridiculous, she thought to herself. You're a grown woman. Emboldened, she pressed on. The slamming of a door to her side, however, quickly wiped away the little courage she had mustered. It was just the wind going through the house. I must've left the front door ajar. Yes, that's it. Soumili walked a few more steps before she flinched once more when she caught her reflection in a mirror. For a fraction of a second, she thought there was nothing amiss, then to her horror she realised that the face looking back at her was not her own. In the mirror a woman with her head half-bowed was staring at Soumili intently. Her whole body held a strange bluish tinge as though she was an image on the screen of a television set that needed its contrast adjusting. In spite of how terrified she was, Soumili reached out to touch the mirror, her hand quivering. It must be a trick. This can't be real.

Before her fingernails came within an inch of the mirror, the apparition grew larger in size. Enraged, it let out a dreadful scream and lifted up its arms as if to strangle Soumili. The mirror then suddenly fell forwards, and Soumili was only just able to move out of the way in time as it smashed against the floor. Silence enveloped the house. Soumili stayed statuesque, her arms raised over her face in a defensive position. She did not know how long she stood there for, but only when she heard Harmesh enter the front door did she move once again.

*

The phone rang whilst Barun and Sukhbir were having dinner. Since he had reached the island, Barun's appetite had been poor, and he had barely touched his meal despite having spent almost an hour preparing it. As such, Barun insisted that it was he who answered the phone rather than Sukhbir.

'Hello?'

'Barun, it's me,' said Jenny. 'Can I meet you?'

'Of course,' he replied. 'Where and when?'

'As soon as possible,' Jenny said, her tone serious. 'If you leave your cottage and walk right for a minute or two, you'll see some railings. There's some stairs down to the beach there. Meet me there in ten minutes.'

The call ended, and Barun went off to collect his coat. After he had informed Sukhbir of where he was going, Barun departed. The temperature was markedly cooler than it had been mid- afternoon, though it was still agreeable. Jenny arrived punctually at the foot of the stairs.

'I'm sorry if I was rather blunt on the phone,' she said. 'I believe there is someone in the station, one of my own officers, reporting the progress of this case to my superiors without my say so.'

They started to amble down the path which ran along the beach.

'It is terrible that anyone would go behind your back in that manner.'

Jenny shrugged. 'In some ways, I'm not annoyed with them. This is an unusual case, and I've opted to bring in outside help. I cannot complain if my commanding officers want to scrutinise my decisions.'

'Well, let us hope that we can put an end to this all as quickly as possible, if only to get these people off your back,' Barun said.

'I'm presuming you haven't had much of a chance to go through the files I had dropped off for you.'

When Barun had returned to the cottage after fetching the deceased man's book, Sukhbir had announced to him that two policemen had delivered some documents and photographs that were of interest to them both. To his surprise, Barun found on the dining table a cardboard box that was over a foot in height.

'I have read a few of the files,' Barun said. 'Though you had told me the pathologist's findings, the pictures of the body did take me aback.'

Jenny briefly looked out in the direction of the sea. 'Oh, yes, the marks are even clearer on those photographs. Mind, they pale in comparison to the slides; I've had a few sleepless nights thinking about those.'

'I'm yet to view them through the projector.' Barun took his sunglasses from his pocket and put them on. 'Going back to the report, theoretically, someone may have assailed the man before his fall, applying enough pressure on his throat to bring out the marks. The issue with this theory, however, is that there were witnesses who saw no one else there. Could he then have choked himself? Possibly, but the sheer number of petechiae spots on his face indicates a level of force which no person could inflict upon themselves without use of a noose.'

Jenny gave a glimmer of a smile. 'Am I sensing that you have another theory?'

'I do, but it is not one that your superiors would entertain,' Barun said. 'The late man's partner handed me a book that contained hundreds of drawings he had made of the same woman. I believe that he had come into contact with a spirit that was at least in part responsible for his death.'

'Do you know anything about this spirit?' she asked.

'At the moment, I can say that I know next to nothing about them other than that they are deceitful.' Barun stopped in his tracks. 'This spirit may be even more dangerous than anything I have ever come across.

Along with the pathologists report, I also read two police reports from last year regarding two separate falls from the cliff. Unfortunately, I saw that there were no post-mortems in those cases so I cannot do a full comparison, but there are some clear similarities between them and the case related to the death of Adrian Worthington. As we first feared, I am now confident that the same spirit has been responsible for multiple deaths.'

Jenny stood in silence for a while, her lips pursed and her hands on her hips. 'Are there any preventative measures that I can be putting in place?'

'Though part of me is tempted to recommend putting in place deterrents to stop anyone from accessing that area of the cliffs, in practice that is easier said than done. Also, I cannot promise that that would lessen the chance of attacks. No, all I can suggest is that you continue to remain vigilant.'

They resumed their walk, though neither of them spoke for more than a minute.

'I must admit that before you arrived I had my doubts whether I had called you out for no reason.' Jenny gave a sharp laugh to herself. 'Safe to say that I don't have any doubts now.'

'Even if you had been mistaken, at least I would have been able to visit this wonderful island,' Barun said cheerfully.

'Yes, it truly is a beautiful place.' Jenny craned her neck up to look at the cliffs. 'I wanted to work somewhere peaceful after living in the hubbub of London, I really did.

Never did I imagine that such horrible things could happen in a sleepy place like this.' She shook her head, seemingly in a reaction to a distressing thought. 'You mentioned a book that belonged to the deceased, didn't you? I would like you to hand it over once you have finished with it, please.'

'Of course,' Barun said. 'If you would like to speak in private again, please do not hesitate to contact me, inspector.'

'Thank you.' She gave a smile that quickly faded. 'Guess I better get back to the station. Are you coming back this way?'

'No, I think I will wander for a bit longer. There is much I wish to mull over.'

*

For the second time in a row, Soumili had an appalling night's sleep. On her shift she was asked to take a blood sample, and it was a small wonder that she was able to keep her hand steady throughout the process. When she went to hand the sample in at the administration desk, Soumili's eyelids became even heavier as she leaned against the counter whilst waiting for a staff member to appear. By the time someone did emerge from the back office, Soumili was practically half-asleep.

She realised that she could not go on this way so walked to the bathroom to freshen up. When she entered the room she felt her heart leap; in her tiredness, it had not entered her mind that there would be mirrors above the sinks. Hurriedly, she strode to the nearest tap and turned its handle, all the while averting her gaze from the mirror above. She waited until the water was almost overflowing from her cupped hands before splashing it on to her face. The water was icy, and for a couple of minutes it seemed to have had the desired effect, but by the time Soumili had dabbed away the droplets by using a paper towel, a deep tiredness took hold of her once more. Two nurses from another ward entered. Soumili was quite pleased that they did not pay any notice to her as the two were far too busy chatting incessantly. Whilst the two women were applying their makeup, Soumili overheard part of their conversation.

'. . . seeing that psychiatrist on the eighth floor – Doctor Garcia I think he's called – because she's been having a terrible time of it of late with her father dying and all,' one of the nurses said.

'Poor woman. She doesn't deserve any of that,' the other said, her cheerful tone utterly inappropriate to the sentiment.

Her friend gave a dismissive wave of her hand. 'I'm sure she'll be fine. Well, yesterday I was talking with. . . '

As Soumili left the bathroom, she glanced at her watch. Twenty minutes until lunchtime. Never before had she sought help for her mental health, but she knew she needed to talk to someone. Though she had told Harmesh of what she had seen, her husband had been quick to dismiss the whole experience; according to him, the woman in the mirror had been nothing more than a hallucination brought on by sleep deprivation. Soumili, however, could not accept this view.

He had not looked into those horrid eyes, and neither had he heard that scream that almost felt like it was still ringing in her ears. Nurses on her ward were given forty-five minutes for their lunch break which Soumili reckoned was ample time to find the doctor's office. Unfortunately, she had not taken into consideration that she had never visited the uppermost floor of the hospital. The hallways were reminiscent of a rabbit warren; it was easy for one to become disorientated whilst wandering through the dingy corridors. By pure luck, she eventually stumbled across his office. There was a brass sign on the door bearing the name of another doctor, though above this there was a sticker on which "Doctor Garcia" was written in blue ink. There was only a third of her lunch break left now, but this did not deter her from knocking on the door.

'Come in,' said a polished voice.

Balding and with a bushy moustache, a middle-aged man was sat at a desk peeling an apple with a pen knife. He peered over his glasses at her. 'If you are my half one, you are frightfully early.'

'Oh, that's not me.' Soumili gently closed the door behind herself. 'Are you Doctor Garcia?'

'That's what it says on the door. . . well, that and the name of my predecessor, though I have been assured that a handyman is supposed to be finally taking that down this week.' His gaze drifted back to his apple. 'Can I help you?'

'I've just started working here this—'

'Have you? Where's your name badge?' he interjected.

Soumili had changed out of her uniform at the start of her break, and she remembered now that she had left her identification badge in her locker along with her work clothes.

'It's in my locker,' she said. 'I've come to see you because I'd like to talk with a professional.

I'm having problems with. . . with. . . ' Soumili's eyes started to well up, and she fought vainly to hold her tears back.

The doctor's demeanour changed in an instant. Leaping to his feet, he put down what he was holding then moved to put an arm around Soumili. 'Good gracious, please take a seat.'

Wiping her tears from her cheeks, Soumili sat down and the doctor pulled his chair away from his desk so that he could sit opposite to her.

'Feel free to tell me as little or as much as you want,' he said in a compassionate tone of voice.

Soumili spoke both freely and quickly. Nodding as he listened, the doctor rarely asked questions, and his expression did not change even when she spoke of the phantom in the mirror. When she had finished, he entwined his fingers. 'I will not lie to you by saying that three or four sessions of therapy and a handful of tablets will address your condition. You swear blind that what you saw was real, and I am not here to say that it wasn't, but we must examine whether your mind created these monsters to protect you in some way.'

Soumili gave a snort. 'Protect me? I've been barely able to sleep or eat the past two days.'

'I am just suggesting that maybe you saw something that was so heartbreaking or disturbing that your mind rejected it entirely and told you that what you had seen was instead something supernatural.' The doctor leaned forwards in his chair ever-so-slightly. 'Let me give you an example: I once supported a lady who had a deep fondness for her cat. One day her poor pet died, yet she could not accept this. So rather than bury her cat and move on with her life, she continued to fill its food bowl whilst leaving the animal to rot in her living room. Eventually, she could no longer go on pretending, and the grief that came over her was all the more terrible because of her initial denial.'

Soumili mulled over his suggestion for a moment. 'I suppose it could be that,' she said unsurely, 'but I have no idea what I could have witnessed.'

'Then we will have to talk further to find out.' He craned his neck to look at the clock on his desk. 'Alas, that is for another time. I have an opening at half five tomorrow afternoon if you are free then.'

'I am, and thank you, Doctor Garcia,' she said. 'I must say that I feel a little better already.'

'I'm happy to hear that.' He gave a warm smile then walked to his desk to pick up a card. 'My details are on this should you ever need to contact me outside of work hours.'

As she took the card, Soumili caught sight of the time. 'Oh, I really need to get back to work. Thanks again.'

She dashed from the room, yet she could not find the elevator so instead took the stairs. When she had finished going down the first flight of stairs, Soumili stopped and looked back on herself. She was not sure why she did this because she had not heard a noise, and she shook her head to herself before pressing on.

*

It had been a lonely day. While Sukhbir remained upstairs relentlessly studying the peculiar book, Barun was left to his own devices on the ground floor. He poured all his attention that day into examining the various files and documents that were within the box that had been delivered to the cottage. During his brief spell as a police officer in Kanpur, he had trained under a captain who was considered by many to be eccentric in his approach to policing, though Barun was not among his critics and in fact believed that the man's techniques were wholly innovative. Barun, a young man of twenty at that time, was also a great admirer of his commanding officer's work ethic. The captain had a firm belief that every single piece of evidence, no matter how insignificant it appeared to be on first viewing, should be examined by an officer for at least an hour. This invariably led to the experienced policeman working long shifts, and even now Barun could vividly picture him hunched over his tiny desk with a set of tweezers between his thumb and forefinger. Though Barun thought scrutinising evidence for this length of time to be excessive, he still followed his former mentor's example to a great extent.

Every single page of the files he read over three times, pausing after he had reached the bottom of the page on each occasion to let the information fully sink in. It did not take an outstanding detective, however, to notice one thing everyone who had fallen from the cliffs had in common: they had all been male. This in itself was in some ways not a surprise as men statistically were more likely to commit suicide than woman, but the fact that over the last twenty years everyone that had been found on the rocks had been of the same gender was most unusual. The other similarity that Barun perceived in the cases was not so obvious to him at first. All the men that had died had had partners. Not all the dead men's partners had been interviewed, but those that had gave varying accounts of how the men had acted preceding their untimely ends. Some had spoken of uncharacteristic behaviours such as going days without talking. Most of those that had been interviewed, however, had not noticed any changes at all. On the face of it, Barun understood perfectly why these tragedies had been considered for so long as either acts of suicides or misadventures. There were only the merest of suggestions that something not of this world had played a part in their demises. A brother of one of the men had told the police that he had witnessed a "shadow" following his sibling as he had departed from his home a matter of hours before he had died, but this account was but a single sentence which was buried within a statement that was at least six hundred words long, and likely interpreted as simple metaphor. This report was dated 19th August 1959.

He sighed as he closed the folder. Leaning back in his chair, he pensively ran his tongue along his bottom lip. Barun's vision was cloudy from tiredness, but he did not yet want to stop for the night. He languidly craned his neck to look over at the projector – a battered, old machine with a cord that had exposed wires – that the police had provided for him. He pulled himself away from the comfort of his chair and found a table to rest the projector upon. Meticulously, Barun then slotted the slides into the machine in order of date then switched it on. Realising that his arm was partly blocking the beam, he moved to one side to examine the first slide.

This was the first time that he had seen a picture of Mister Worthington alive, although few details could be made out as the photograph had been taken at a fair distance and it was also in sepia. The man had been wearing a flat cap and coat at the time, and in this picture nothing appeared untoward other than that he was stood approximately eight feet away from a sudden drop. Barun changed to the next slide. He felt the hairs on the back of his neck stand on end as he stared at the image that was being projected. At this moment, it must have been clear to Brian that the man he was photographing was about to die. With his head bowed, the man had moved right to the edge and by this point only one of his feet remained on the ground.

Adjusting his glasses, Barun moved himself closer to the image. A shadowy figure was positioned behind the man. The longer he stared at this shape, the clearer it seemed to become. Soon, he could see that they were a woman wearing a flowing dress, and that their hands were wrapped around the back of the man's neck. Unflinching, Barun watched in shock as the woman gradually turned her head to look directly at him with her pale eyes. The carousel flitted from one picture to the next, yet her presence now dominated every single photograph. The light of the projector cut out briefly and when it returned Mister Worthington was no longer present in the picture yet she remained, her whole body now facing towards Barun. Again the light of the machine went out but this time it did not return on its own accord, so Barun span round and gave the projector a sharp tap using his knuckles. The light came back on.

The grainy image now being displayed was of a wooded area with a building in the distance. Barun thought that he recognised the place, but he did not have a chance to examine the location for very long. The woman reappeared. The phantom now stood at the centre of the image and was only visible from the waist upwards. She was a dreadful sight. The flesh around her mouth had rotted away to the extent that her teeth were exposed, whilst her face was covered in skin tears. Her eyes, however, were the feature that unnerved Barun the most: they were utterly colourless and fixed on him. For what felt to Barun like an eternity, he stared into his foe's eyes. The light flickered, and all of a sudden she was no longer in the picture, and instead the phantom was in the very room, her groping hands outstretched towards Barun's throat. She stank of death. Letting out a horrid shriek, she rushed at him at incredible speed.

Quickly, Barun lunged for the projector's wire, and with one swift yank, he pulled it from the socket. Darkness. Barun stayed motionless as he assessed the situation. His shirt was soaked with sweat and it clung to his skin, whilst his heart was racing. Though in the blackness he could see nothing other than the vague outlines of the room's furniture, Barun could tell that the dead woman was no longer present. Fumbling around, he found the light switch and turned it on. In his panic, he had knocked the projector off the table, and it now lay upside down on the floor. He picked it up and checked to see if it had been damaged in the same moment that Sukhbir burst into the room.

'What's wrong?' he asked, gasping for air.

'She was here,' Barun replied dreamily. 'I think she intended to kill me.'

Sukhbir started to frantically look around. 'What? Who was here?'

'The one responsible for all this woe.' Barun gave a vague gesture at nothing in particular. 'Never have I known of a spirit capable of projecting themselves to an area that they do not haunt through means of a photograph,' he said, sniffing at the air. 'Can you smell that?'

After momentarily raising his nose, Sukhbir began to wretch and placed the back of his hand over his nostrils. 'That's terrible! Smells like a rotten body!'

'I first perceived it when she manifested in the room; it is truly remarkable that it's still present even though she's no longer here.' Barun returned the machine to the table. 'That Brian boy had captured a picture of her with his camera, and Jenny had got someone to make a slide of the image. It goes without saying that I did not expect to find myself in peril when I flicked that switch.'

Sukhbir cast a wary glance at the projector. 'Are we sure that it is safe to be near it?'

'Oh, I think so,' Barun said. 'She vanished the moment I pulled the plug out, so I am guessing we won't come to harm unless we turn it back on.'

'Well, let us avoid doing that.' Sukhbir frowned. 'I was actually about to come to find you regarding another matter.'

'And what is that?'

'I don't have an explanation of how it happened, but the book I have been studying has changed,' Sukhbir said. 'Come, I'll show you.'

The two men headed to Sukhbir's room in which he had been studying the mysterious book. 'There were some pages towards the back of the book that were completely blank. Well, when I looked at them again a few minutes ago. . . ' Pulling back the chair that was at the desk, he signalled for his colleague to sit down. 'Just have a look for yourself, Barun.'

He complied and sat at the desk in order to examine the book. His eyes widened when he came to the pages that Sukhbir had been talking about. Written in cursive were several diary entries, the first of which was dated 3rd July 1940. Barun read from the first passage: *Alexander and I were meant to be together. All those months of hoping that the planets would suddenly align in my favour and make him notice me. Now our wedding night will be under the light of a blood red moon. . . I am told this only happens every once a year! I couldn't be happier.*

The entries continued in much the same vein, though there were the odd lines here and there that suggested that something was amiss. After he had finished reading the entries, Barun took off his glasses and rubbed the brow of his nose.

'What are your thoughts?' Sukhbir asked.

'I was hoping that at some point she would have given us her name, but, alas, we are not in luck.' Barun ran his finger down the page that the book was open on. 'As for what she did write down, it does not tell us much. Judging by the ink and the handwriting, it does appear, though, that the person who wrote this also wrote those earlier passages that were in Aramaic and the other languages.'

Sukhbir breathed out through his nose. 'But why? Why would one include their own sentimental thoughts alongside rituals transcribed in an ancient tongue?'

'Rituals,' Barun muttered to himself. 'Isn't it true that some cultures over the years have performed rituals under a blood moon?'

Grinning, Sukhbir clicked his fingers. 'That's right. Over the centuries, some have believed a blood moon to be an ill omen, though there are those that consider the event to be the opposite.'

'So it would seem that she wanted to make certain that their marriage would be a blissful one by having the ceremony during this particular celestial occurrence,' Barun said. 'Well, that is a theory at least. I do think that we can safely assume, however, that it is no coincidence that this writing appeared at the same time that the spirit tried to attack me.'

'So she was the one who wrote this book?' Sukhbir asked.

Barun shrugged and took a cigar from his pocket. 'That would stand to reason,' he said, lighting the cigar.

CHAPTER SIX

The sound of the front door opening and closing caused Harmesh to look up from his book. He did not need to look at his wife's expression for long to determine that she was in distress.

'What happened? Are you okay?' he asked, standing up. 'You look worried.'

She shook her head and pointed out of the window. 'Someone has been following me; it might've been that guy who was taking our pictures.'

'Is he still out there?'

'I don't know,' she said with a huff. 'I ran away.'

Harmesh lifted his hands and placed them on her shoulders. 'He's just a boy who likes his photography.'

'Yes, one who knows where I live and now where I work.' Soumili pursed her lips. 'Why's he taking my pictures?'

'Because you're so beautiful.' Laughing, Harmesh playfully pinched her cheek.

He regretted this action when she grimaced then looked to her side. 'It's not funny,' she said in a dry tone.

'Okay, I can see that,' Harmesh said. 'Do you want me to report him?'

Soumili paused for a moment in thought. 'Yes.'

'Fine.' Harmesh gave a half-smile. 'I'll get onto that in the morning because tonight I have a surprise for you.'

Soumili's face brightened ever-so-slightly. 'You do?'

'I certainly do. I was having a pleasant chat with a greengrocer earlier on today, and he happened to mention that he had tickets for a show that he could no longer attend. Anyway, I bought them off him and tonight we are seeing. . . the ballet!'

Soumili gasped in excitement. 'Seriously?'

'Yes, but you better change quickly.' Harmesh looked at his watch. 'It starts in just over an hour.'

Harmesh was confident that a trip to the theatre would prove to be the perfect tonic to his wife's anxieties, and he was glad to find that she was back to her old self before they had even set off. From time to time during the performance, he would glance over to her simply to see the delighted look on her face. Harmesh was not a great admirer of ballet, but he did not mind in the slightest sitting through it as he knew how happy Soumili was to be there. She slept for practically the whole ride home, and Harmesh needed to wake her up with a gentle tap on the knee once they arrived. After changing out of his formal clothing, he made himself a drink then switched on the television set. A tank left a cloud of dust in its wake as it raced across the screen whilst the reporter told the viewer of the recent revolution in Afghanistan.

Above him Harmesh could hear the sound of Soumili running a bath for herself. Positioning one the armchairs closer to the screen, he sat down and breathed a content sigh. After briefly dozing off, he was roused by a call from outside. It was Soumili's voice. Grabbing his cap from the stand, Harmesh put it on and hurried out into the night. There was a chill in the air which was intensified by a wind blowing in from the sea. Harmesh stared aghast at the scene before him. Pivoting on the garden path with her arms flailing by her side, Soumili was laughing hysterically to herself.

'Soumili?'

She continued to laugh as she beckoned him to follow her. 'Come here, Harmesh,' she said. It was definitely her voice that he heard, but it held a peculiar echo as though she was speaking from within a tunnel. There was quite clearly something greatly awry with his wife, but Harmesh did not have a chance to stop to think because she had already gone through the gate and left his sight.

He pursued her. 'Where are you going?'

*

A deep bellow from outside caused Barun and Sukhbir to spring to their feet. Barun ran straight for a telescope that was situated in front of the window.

'What on earth was that?' Sukhbir asked.

Barun knew exactly where to point the telescope towards. A mist had set in around the area, yet fortunately it was not too thick. Through the lens Barun made out a very animated figure; they were stood on the cliff edge.

'Get the police,' he told his assistant before bolting for the door.

With no street lamps to light his way, Barun had to rely purely on his instincts as he ran. Dashing over a field and then through a wood, Barun scratched his hand on a low-lying branch and almost tripped over twice before he reached the cliff. His stomach churned when he saw that the person looming over the edge was not the same one that he had seen through the telescope. A young man was pointing his camera downwards in the direction of the rocks. Running to this stranger's side, Barun looked over the edge and saw no sign of life.

'Did you see what happened? Who was it?' Barun blurted out.

The young man whimpered before he spoke. 'I didn't do anything! I was just taking pictures!'

Anger, an unfamiliar emotion to Barun, came over him and he grabbed the man by the collar of his coat. 'Come with me!' he yelled, pulling him away from the cliffs.

*

The sun was just starting to rise, though the sky to the east was so cloudy that it was almost imperceptible. Soumili had lost track of time and did not know how long she had been vacantly staring out at the waters. In front of her there was a diminutive, knee-high railing that someone in their wisdom had decided was a suitable barrier to stop people from wandering onto an embankment which ran down to the sea.

She started at the sound of a woman's voice. 'Mrs. Banerjee,' Inspector Jones said as she approached.

'Anything?' Soumili asked, and she perceived the desperation in her tone.

'I'm sorry.' The policewoman shook her head. 'We still haven't found any signs of him, though our boats have just started to comb the area again. But I must warn you that because it was high tide when. . . '

Soumili could not bring herself to look the woman in the eye for it felt in that moment as though to do so would confirm to her that this was not all just some horrific nightmare that she was yet to wake from. 'Okay,' she said feebly.

'Did he leave a note or a letter?' the inspector asked.

'He wouldn't do anything like that!' Soumili bit back, though her anger faded almost instantly, and she began to sob again.

'I'm sorry, I just needed to ask,' the inspector said in a markedly gentler tone. 'Look, we have two eyewitnesses who are helping us out with the investigation, and we have no plans to call off the search yet. As things stand, there is still a chance that we might find him.'

Wiping her eyes with her sleeves, Soumili looked back to the waves lashing at the shoreline. She pictured her husband lying inside a remote cove, semi-conscious and muttering her name, but then her thoughts turned to a darker possibility. On their honeymoon Soumili had gone for a swim in the sea whilst they were staying at a cottage in south-western England, yet she had found the waters to be bitterly cold and only lasted minutes before returning to the beach. Last night in Corvid's Head, the temperatures had been far cooler than on that particular day that Soumili had gone swimming. How could anyone spend an entire night in freezing waters? As hard as she tried, Soumili could not expel the question from her mind.

*

It felt as though he was trapped miles below the surface in some kind of subterranean bomb shelter. Of course Brian knew that this was not the case, though it was still a sensation that had persisted since the moment he had been shoved into the tiny cell. There were only three doors between Brian and freedom, yet to him that might as well have been a thousand. An acrid smell of disinfectant clung to the air, and the walls were tacky to the touch. His thoughts turned to his mother. He was not concerned so much about her feelings, more the rage that she would surely unleash once he had been released from this miserable place; that was, if he was released.

Sat on the cell's uncomfortable bed, Brian stared blankly at the wall trying to figure out why the tiles were so familiar to him. Several minutes later he realised that the changing room in his school had had the same tiles. He did not have happy memories of that place, but at least his friend had looked out for him. She had been with him for as long as he could remember. Sometimes, when people upset him, she would punish them. There were times he hated her, and there were times he adored her. The other day he had lost consciousness on his porch and woken up in a field miles away from his home. Once he had brushed himself off and got to his feet, she had calmed Brian by telling him that she had been watching over him. Nothing bad would happen to Brian whilst she was with him. Whether he believed this or not did not seem to really matter to Brian.

The shutter of the door slid across to reveal two hazel eyes under a thick brow.

'You want a drink?' asked a gruff voice.

Brian cleared his throat. 'Water. . . p-please.'

He could not be certain that the officer had heard his request for they drew the shutter back across without saying another word. Raising his feet onto the bed, Brian hugged his legs tightly. All this while her voice had been getting louder and louder in his head.

Empty your mind, she told him over and over again.

Brian pressed his hands over his ears so hard that they started to hurt. There was nothing, however, he could do to stop the voice. It was almost like she was in the room now, hunched over him and watching his every move.

For the briefest of moments, his thoughts turned to the man who had grabbed him last night on the cliff edge. He did not know who the man was, though Brian could tell that he was different to all the others. Maybe he was actually someone who could understand what he was going through. Who knows, maybe he could even help him. She was not happy that he was thinking about someone who was not her, and she let him know this by causing a searing headache to spread across his temple. Brian yelped in pain. Hoping that the police officers in the corridor did not hear his cry, Brian at last started to focus on her voice and soon all the pain faded away.

*

Jenny arrived back at the station to find Sergeant Stepney pacing back and forth in the entrancc hall as he waited for her to return.

'Ma'am, we have him in cell three,' he said, frowning. 'I can bring him to the interview room when you are ready.'

'Right.' Jenny took off her cap. 'I think it's best for everyone if we get this out of the way.'

The room in which they interviewed suspects and witnesses was a dingy, little place that lay in the centre of the building. Though they had tried many ways to warm it, the room was always cold, and in the winter months the officers found that even electric heaters did little to ward off the chill. Jenny checked the cassettes, whilst the sergeant went to collect Brian Dawson. The room became lighter for a fleeting moment as the door was opened then shut again. Placing the young man firmly down in the chair opposite to his superior, the sergeant gave Jenny a perfunctory nod before he left the room. With his head bowed, Brian was trembling profusely. He sat in a twisted posture with his arms held tightly to his sides whilst he kept making a whining sound that was reminiscent of a newborn dog.

Jenny pressed the record button on the machine. 'Commencing interview with suspect Brian Dawson at three minutes past eleven. Inspector Jenny Jones speaking.' She breathed out through her nose before going on. 'Brian, what were you doing at the cliffs last night?'

There was no response from the young man.

'We have a witness who found you on the spot where Harmesh Banerjee was last seen,' she went on. 'Did you push him, Brian?'

'Push,' the boy repeated back in a yelp.

'Is that your answer? I must remind you that this conversation is being recorded and may be used in a court of law,' Jenny said. 'Brian, did you push Harmesh Banerjee?'

'Not me,' he whined. 'Not Brian.'

'Well, then who pushed him, Brian? Do you know their name?' she asked.

Placing his forehead on the table, the young man began to wail. Jenny was confident that Brian knew what had happened last night, but she did not feel comfortable continuing the interview with him in his current state. She was about to call a halt to proceedings when he suddenly stopped with his wailing. Slowly, Brian started to look up. Bulging, blue veins had appeared around his temple, whilst his eyes, his dreadful eyes, were now colourless. There was a part of Jenny that wanted to flee from the room, but she remained seated. After several seconds of staring perplexed at the man, Jenny stopped the cassette. She made a gesture directed at the one-way mirror, hoping that there was someone on the other side. Suddenly, Brian erupted into a tirade, his face etched in fury. He did not speak in a language that Jenny recognised, and if the sergeant had not entered into the room at that exact second to restrain him, Brian would surely have attacked her by lunging across the table.

Trying all the while to regulate her breathing, Jenny followed them and watched as the burly sergeant struggled against the man who must have been only three quarters of his height. One of the constables, noticing the commotion, emerged from a side room and helped Sergeant Stepney to force young Brian Dawson back into his cell. Jenny had known the sergeant for a number of years, and she knew of few people as good as him when it came to hiding one's emotions; however, the look on his face as he pulled away from the cell door was one of unbridled consternation. There was only one thing that Jenny felt she could do.

*

He had been asleep for but an hour when the phone rang. Jenny had not given him that much information, but her brief account of the interview of Brian Dawson was enough for Barun to sit bolt upright from his makeshift bed. After pouring himself a cup of tepid coffee from a percolator that Sukhbir had left out, Barun made his way to the station. Entering the building, he sensed a bizarre aura as though he had walked into a place of pure misery that was devoid of any form of happiness.

He started to feel hopeless, questioning whether he could stop the entity that was tormenting the residents of the island. Pausing in the foyer to focus his mind, Barun was able to summon the resolve he needed to ward off these doubts. He pressed on and found Jenny waiting for him.

'Thank you for coming. Something very strange has happened to Brian. He was fine one second then the next. . .' she trailed off whilst making a circular motion with her hands. 'You best follow me.'

She led him to a gloomy corridor with a row of reinforced doors running down one side. Jenny stopped by one of the doors. 'He's in here. I've got to go to see to something, but I'll be back in a minute. Just pull the shutter across if you want to start talking with him.'

The inspector's footsteps echoed along the hallway as she departed. Lifting his hand, he slid the shutter across and peered inside the cell. Brian was sat on a bed hugging his legs with his face buried in his knees. His belt and shoes had clearly been confiscated, and he was also missing his shirt. Sat in his vest and shorts, he cut a pathetic figure and did not appear like someone capable of hurting a fly.

'Brian? It's me, Barun. We met last night,' he said through the opening. 'There have been some concerns about you. How are you feeling at the minute?'

Gradually, Brian raised his head. He wore a malevolent smirk upon his face, and his eyes were just as Jenny had described to him over the phone. Unnerved by the pale eyes that were watching him, Barun started to step away, but before his back foot had fully connected with the floor, the cell door opened. Brian shot towards Barun then grabbed him by the throat. Though he was scrawny, the young man had astonishing strength, and Barun felt like he was close to passing out within seconds of being grabbed. He tried to grapple with his assailant, but Barun's hands went straight through him as though he was attempting to take a hold of thin air.

'What's wrong, Barun?' Jenny's voice asked.

Barun blinked and saw that the door was still closed with Brian locked behind it. Nursing his throat with one hand, Barun linked arms with Jenny and pulled her away.

'Do not let anyone enter that room,' he said in a hoarse voice. 'No one should open that door under any circumstances.'

The inspector gave a bemused smile. 'Barun, I cannot do that; unless we charge him today, we've got to let him go.'

'Then charge him,' Barun said bluntly.

'But do you think he actually did it?' she asked.

Barun did not answer, and he continued to rub his throat.

Placing her hands on her hips, Jenny squinted her eyes as she looked at him as though she was trying to read his mind. 'What on Earth happened to you back there?'

Barun glanced at the door and, concerned that they could be overheard, he ushered the police officer further away from the cell before he spoke. 'It is my belief that Brian is possessed.'

She raised an eyebrow. 'Possessed? Like the woman we came across in London all those years ago?'

'Yes. . . well, sort of,' Barun said. 'Whatever is within Brian is not what you might call a typical spirit. Last night, I was just starting to form a theory, but this revelation has blown that apart. I'm going to have to expand my research.' He reached into his pocket for a cigar. 'Brian Dawson is a great danger to anyone who comes into contact with him. If he was to walk free now, there is no guessing what he could do. I appreciate that you must carry out your duties as a police officer, though I implore you to find a way to keep him locked away until I know what we are dealing with.'

Jenny nodded. 'Just be as quick as you can, right? His mother is due in any minute now, and I can hardly explain to her that her son is being controlled by something unspeakable.'

As he headed out of the station, Barun could not help but feel a shade of guilt for he had lied by omission. He had an idea what was inhabiting Brian, but he did not want to panic the inspector by telling her until he knew for sure.

*

It was the first time that Soumili had slept in nearly forty hours. This was not a deep sleep, rather the type that feels as though one has merely closed their eyes for an extended period of time. With none of her friends or family on the island, Soumili had turned to Doctor Garcia for support. She had, however, found his suggestions to be altogether unhelpful, so she had then decided to make the difficult call to her mother to tell her that her husband was missing, presumed dead. Having relocated to England largely so that she could attend her daughter's wedding, Soumili's mother, once she had recovered from the shocking news, had insisted that she would come immediately to the island. Unfortunately, she first needed to get a bus from Warwickshire to the port meaning that she would not arrive until the following day.

Soumili closed her eyes once more, and the next time she opened them day had turned to night. It had not occurred to her before she had lain down upon her bed to close the curtains, and all that could be seen through the panes was utter darkness. The grandfather clock in the living room struck eleven o'clock. A horrible sensation then met her left wrist, Soumili recoiling and looking to her side. It had felt like a hand had been placed upon her, one that was leathery and as cold as snow.

Such was her grief that she had almost forgotten about the terrible woman in the smashed mirror, but in that moment alone in the house, she could think of nothing else. She sat upright and looked around. A thud came from her bedroom door. This was swiftly followed by another, though this second thud was noticeably louder. Beneath the window, two chairs slid across the flooring before they both became upturned. Soumili threw her hands over ears as she rocked back and forth. This isn't real. It's all in my head, she told herself. Then she saw her. The reason that Soumili had not noticed her before was that the spectre was in a particularly dark area in the corner of the room. As Soumili's eyes adjusted to the blackness, her terror only increased for gradually she was able to make out more and more of its features. It was dead, or rather it should have been. Soumili believed it to be the same being that she had seen in the mirror, though the thing that was now lurking in the shadows of her bedroom was more decayed than it had appeared the other day.

Soumili shut her eyes. Though her palms were still pressed against her ears, she could still make out footsteps. The creature's approach was slow and methodical like a predator stalking its prey. After the seventh or eighth step, there was silence. After a while, Soumili dared to open her eyes. The phantom was gone without a trace. Removing her hands from her ears, she started to shuffle herself towards the bottom of her bed to peep over the edge in order to check that it was definitely gone. Suddenly, the dead woman sprang up and darted at her. Soumili, with no way to escape, let out a scream and raised her arms to defend herself. She did not know whether it was her shriek or something else that caused the creature to vanish, but this time when she opened her eyes Soumili was certain that it was no longer in her room.

Once she had plucked up the courage, Soumili ventured downstairs, and she spent the night inside a walk-in cupboard with her back pressed up against the door for it was the only place in the house in which she believed that the spectre could not easily reach her. Once morning came, she frantically got changed then began the long walk to the police station. Despite the beauty of the scenery, the journey was gruelling. Every time a wall came in sight she would watch it intently until she had passed it in fear that the horrible being would clamber over it before assailing her.

An officious policeman initially prevented her from going any further than the station's front desk, but he swiftly changed his stance once he looked up from his paperwork and saw her scowling face. Trudging off, he fetched Inspector Jones.

'Mrs. Banerjee, how are you holding up?' the inspector asked.

Soumili threw a glance over to a group of nearby officers. 'Can we speak somewhere a bit more private?'

The inspector ushered her through a set of double doors which led to a quiet corridor.

'Something is wrong in the house.' Only after Soumili had spoken did she realise that she must have come across as rather brusque.

'Have you had another trespasser?' the inspector asked.

'No.' Soumili shook her head, but then she had a sudden thought. 'Wait, yes. I need someone to come to check the house.'

'We can arrange that.' Inspector Jones frowned. 'Tell me what happened, Mrs. Banerjee.' Spluttering, Soumili tried to find a way to describe the night's events. 'I've seen chairs and doors move by themselves. . . and there's this woman; she keeps vanishing then reappearing later.'

Soumili looked into the policewoman's eyes and perceived doubt in them. 'You don't believe me, do you?'

'It's not that,' she replied in an unconvincing manner. 'I'm just aware that you've been through a lot lately. Sit down with me.'

Though in her frustration Soumili felt like storming out of the building, she begrudgingly complied with the inspector's request.

'Look, I have been working with an investigator who deals with. . . the abnormal,' Inspector Jones went on. 'In fact, you have already met him. If you think it might help, I can contact him to see if he would consider having a look round.'

Soumili mulled over the inspector's suggestion. In truth, she had not entered the station with a clear idea of what she actually wanted the police to do about the disturbing goings-on in her house, but now that she sat there she appreciated that there was little they could do other than send someone out to inspect the property.

'Okay.' Soumili nodded before she turned the conversation to her missing husband.

*

Once he came within a hundred metres of the house, Barun stopped in his tracks. When the spectre had appeared to him on the night he was viewing the slides, he had vaguely recognised a building that she had been standing outside, though he had been too distracted at the time to rack his brain in order to figure out the reason why the place was so familiar to him. Now Barun realised that the grainy image that had been displayed was of the House on the Cliff, the home of Soumili Banerjee.

During the course of his investigation into the mysterious deaths on the island, Barun had come across several incidents or pieces of evidence that in some way shape or form were linked to the house. The fact that the dead woman had chosen to appear at this particular setting proved for certain that these links were not merely coincidences. The most recent incident which had links to the house was, of course, the disappearance of Harmesh Banerjee who had now been missing for over forty-eight hours and had moved into the property with his wife only a matter of days ago.

Continuing on, Barun opened the gate and entered the garden. As he walked, he noticed that his legs seemed to feel weaker with each step, and by the time he reached the door the sensation had spread to his whole body. He could no longer stay on his feet, and with the shred of energy that he had left in his body he deliberately fell backwards onto the freshly cut lawn in order to avoid hitting the stone steps in front of him. This feeling that had come over Barun was not entirely alien to him. Sometimes after he had experienced a vision he would feel altogether drained and require a while to recuperate. What was happening to his body at present, however, was far more intense than anything he had ever faced before. His mouth became very warm, and he tasted the familiar, metallic tang of blood on the back of his tongue. Spitting the blood into his palm, he began to convulse as he fought to stay conscious. After rolling onto his side, Barun poured all his focus into trying to get onto his hands and knees which, to his surprise, he was able to achieve on his first attempt. Languidly raising his head, he caught sight of her. Sat on the steps was the dead woman, her mouth twisted into a mocking grin. Barun could not bear to look at her for very long, and he soon averted his gaze.

'Are you okay? What happened?' a panicked voice asked.

Getting to his feet, Barun discovered that Soumili had run out of the house to check on him. Meanwhile, the spectre who had been seated upon the doorstep had vanished.

'I'm fine.' Barun instinctively plucked a cigar from his pocket. 'I just fell down.'

Though he felt far better now that the horrid being was no longer toying with him, Barun was still a bit light-headed as he entered the house. After he had politely turned down Soumili's offer of a glass of water, they sat down on a sofa.

'Inspector Jones told me that you believe in the paranormal,' she said in a small voice. 'Is that true?'

'It is,' he replied. 'Without wanting to sound too arrogant, I consider myself an expert in the field.'

'Then, Mister Rai, you may have an interest in this house.' She glanced up at the ceiling as though she had heard a noise coming from upstairs. 'Things have happened in this house lately that have both terrified me and perplexed me. There is a woman here that comes and goes. I know that she wishes me ill fortune, though she has never actually hurt me physically, come to think of it. My husband. . . I don't know whether she had a hand in his fall.'

'I believe you are correct, Mrs. Banerjee,' he said softly. 'A woman died here many years ago, and she either refused to pass on to the other side or there is something dreadful stopping her from doing so.'

Soumili's eyes widened. 'Do you think she pushed him?'

'That I cannot be sure of; I saw Harmesh that night from a distance, though he had fallen by the time I arrived at the precipice.'

For a fleeting moment, it appeared as though she was about to start crying, but then her face wrinkled into a stern expression. 'Mister Rai, can you stop her from doing this to anyone else?'

Barun took her by the hand. 'When it comes to that, all I can do is promise you that I will do everything in my power to rid this house of her. My assistant is currently studying that old book which we discovered here, and he is hoping for a breakthrough shortly. In the meantime, is there anywhere else you can stay on the island?'

She vigorously shook her head. 'There is nowhere, and even if there was, I am not leaving my home. I refuse to give up all hope on Harmesh, even if it appears that there are certain people that have decided that he is gone. I had this dream last night that he returned to me, calling my name from the bottom of the stairs. Call me foolish, but I believe that I saw into the future.'

'And who am I to say that you did not.' Barun smiled briefly. 'If I cannot convince you to leave here, however, I do recommend that you find a holy man to see if they can cleanse the house.'

'Someone did try to do just that,' Soumili said. 'His name was Father Paul. He rolled up one day offering to bless the house, but while he was here I went into the back garden to speak with Harmesh, and when I returned inside this priest was gone. Whatever he did, it clearly did not work.'

Barun idly rubbed his chin. 'I think I will attempt to have a word with this man.' He took out his notepad and pen from his trouser pocket then began writing. 'Should you have any further worries, please contact me on this number. My colleague Sukhbir and I are staying in a cottage not too far away from here.'

After the woman had thanked him for his time, Barun promptly departed. On his journey back to his lodgings, Barun's mind was so preoccupied that he almost walked out into oncoming traffic, the blast of the car horn jolting him from his musings.

He entered the cottage to find Sukhbir lingering in the downstairs hallway.

'I was about to come out to look for you,' Sukhbir said, his eyes wild. 'I've just translated a line which I believe goes some way to identifying the source of the problem.'

Barun took in a deep breath. 'Yes?'

'She placed a curse, one that targets men that go near the house.'

'So that explains why all those who have fallen in recent years have been male,' Barun said thoughtfully. 'You get anything else?'

'This curse is like nothing I've seen before.' Sukhbir shuffled uncomfortably on the spot.

'Most victims of curses simply find themselves stricken with ill fortune, yet this ritual summoned a being into our world that chooses an individual then leads them to their doom.'

'This is the being that must have possessed Brian.'

'I would say that it almost certainly is,' Sukhbir said. 'There's more: the being operates in cycles. Before the next harvest moon, it will look to possess a woman then consume her soul before it goes into some kind of hibernation for a year.'

'A harvest moon? Not a blood moon like they had mentioned in that diary entry?'

'Well, I initially thought I had translated the passage incorrectly, but I double-checked my work and am confident that the event that the curse refers to is the harvest moon,'

Sukhbir said. 'I do, however, hope that I'm wrong because I heard on the radio this morning that a harvest moon will occur tomorrow night.'

Half-closing his eyes, Barun leaned against a nearby wall with one hand. 'You know, there is a technique that I can use which may help us. I have been staving off even mentioning it so far as it could give this being an opportunity for this being to see into my mind. A shaman taught me the method many years ago, but I have only ever used it on one occasion.'

'So it is like one of your visions?'

'Yes, except it is more intense and dangerous. That said, it may not necessarily work.' Barun shrugged. 'Whether it's the woman who is haunting the house or this otherworldly being that she once upon a time summoned, one of them is still preventing me from having visions.'

Sighing, Sukhbir folded his arms. 'I don't like the sound of this, to be honest; however, if we don't do something quickly, they'll be another body in the morgue.'

'My thoughts exactly,' Barun said. 'I'll do it in the lounge. Please could you sit facing me, and if you for a second believe that I am in trouble, shake me from my state. If I were you I would also make sure that you are comfortable; this could take some time.'

Though Sukhbir acted in accordance to his wishes, Barun perceived a subtle look of trepidation on his friend's face. After he had had a stiff drink, Barun seated himself in an armchair then lowered his eyelids. The first stage of the process involved him picturing a long tunnel with a door at the end of it. Once he felt like he was ready to continue, he imagined walking down this tunnel and turning the handle of the door. This was the moment in which he would discover whether a spirit would prevent him from going onwards. To his relief, the door opened. His mind was flooded with images. A woman wearing a wedding dress looked out to the ocean. Bodies littered a beach. In the Banerjee's home, a priest threw his hands up to protect himself from an unseen threat. Throughout his trance he felt like he was being watched. He never saw the terrible spirit, though he did sense both its power and its malice. Barun opened his eyes and saw Sukhbir staring back at him.

'How long was I out for?' he asked, rubbing at his brow.

Sukhbir checked his watch. 'Almost three hours. Did it work? What did you see?'

Before he replied, Barun reached for his drink that was upon a coffee table and had a sip of it. 'I felt a strange presence emitting from the cliffs by the Banerjee's house: it was the fiend that was summoned. It's growing in strength. . . becoming more confident. I fear that if it consumes another soul, it will become so powerful that nothing on Earth will be able to stop it. Eventually, its evil may spread across the whole island.' Barun paused for a moment. 'I saw dozens of bodies on the shoreline. Part of me now wonders if the tide has also got something to do with it.'

'That would make a lot of sense; after all, the tide is partially controlled by the moon,' Sukhbir said.

'When is the spring tide?' Barun asked, gesturing to a newspaper that was draped over the arm of the sofa.

After scanning the newspaper for almost a minute, Sukhbir let out a gasp. 'It's this week.'

Barun rubbed at his eye. 'I would like to visit the Banerjee's home again, but this time I will enter a trance. Perhaps being in the epicentre of all this will help to reveal something new.'

*

Yet again, Soumili had a disturbed night. The radio switched itself on at one point, and even though she paced across the living room to turn it off, it continued to blare out some old-timey song: a crackling swing piece. Eventually, she resorted to pulling the plug from the socket. When the doorbell rang in the morning, she flinched at the noise. Because of her tiredness, she had completely forgotten who was visiting her that day. Tears flowing down her face, Soumili threw her arms around her mother and sobbed into her shoulder. Her mother was not a talkative person, and she barely said a word for the first hour that she was in house; however, she eventually started to ask questions, the type that Soumili did not want to answer. Soumili gave vague responses to everything her mother asked her for a while before she was able to change the subject. While her mother was making her a cup of tea, it dawned on Soumili how selfish she had been: by allowing her mother into her home, she had potentially placed her in danger. When her mother returned with their drinks, Soumili attempted to convince her that it may be for the best if she stayed in a hotel, but her mother insisted that she was not going to abandon her only daughter to traipse around a large house on her own whilst she was in mourning.

Peculiarly, Soumili now actually wanted nothing more than to be alone, and she fabricated an illness as an excuse to take to her bedroom. As soon as she entered the room,

Soumili became transfixed on her own reflection in the desk mirror. She sat down and opened her makeup box.

Putting aside all her worries, Soumili began applying her eyeliner and, once she had finished, picked up a lipstick at random. She did know exactly why, but Soumili had this feeling that she needed to prepare for an occasion, one that was going to take place shortly.

*

Following the sudden appearance of the dead woman the last time he ventured to the House on the Cliff, Barun asked on this occasion for Sukhbir to accompany him. Thankfully, they were able to reach the front door without experiencing any issues at all. The door was answered by a middle- aged woman who Barun did not recognise.

She was squinting as though there was a bright light shining in her eyes. 'Yes?'

'Hello. We are helping the police and would like to speak with Soumili,' Sukhbir said.

The woman gave a slow shake of her head. 'She is sleeping at the minute.'

'Ah, well we don't want to disturb her while she is resting.' Barun gave a half-smile. 'In actuality, we just wanted to check the living room for something; it's in relation to Harmesh's disappearance.'

After a moment's thought, she agreed to the request with a nod.

'Can I fetch either of you gentlemen a tea?' she asked once she had shown them inside.

‘Yes, that would be lovely,’ Barun said in a cheery voice.

The second the woman was out of the room, they both sat down.

‘We don’t have much time,’ Sukhbir whispered.

Barun, slightly perturbed that his companion was stating the obvious whilst he was trying to focus on the task at hand, did not respond to him and lowered his eyelids. It usually took him some time to enter a trance, but he began to see past events within seconds of shutting his eyes. Harmesh was sat watching the television. Someone drew him outside. He cared for this person and did not want to see them come to harm. When Harmesh reached the cliff edge, Barun saw who he had been following: it was Soumili. She showed no concern at all to her own wellbeing as she teetered on the precipice, and Harmesh rushed towards her in an ill-fated attempt to pull her away from the danger.

The man cried as he fell; the shout caused Barun to open his eyes.

The middle-aged woman, who told the two investigators that she was Soumili’s mother, returned to the living room with their drinks. They explained that they had found what they were looking, though neither of the men wanted to come across as being rude so they stayed to finish their tea. Once outside, they wandered over to a railing before they started speaking to one another.

‘So? What did you see?’ Sukhbir asked.

Barun produced his lighter and a cigar from his pocket. ‘I saw Harmesh running behind someone on the clifftop.’

‘It was Brian, yes?’

'No, it was a woman. It looked like Soumili,' Barun said.

Sukhbir gave a look of incredulity. 'Soumili? But she told Inspector Jones that she was in the bath at the time. Do you think she had a hand in his death?'

'I think that is unlikely.' Barun lit his cigar. 'Studies have suggested that powerful spirits may have the ability to change their appearance. What if some of the men that have fallen over the years have been lured to the edge in the belief that their partner was in danger?'

'That would certainly explain a lot.' Sukhbir nodded to himself. 'So what now?'

'I'm going to go back to the library.' Barun checked his watch. 'I know we have gone through their archives of local newspapers already, but I want to have a look through the nationals. We have seen firsthand how reserved the people here are: maybe none of the local reporters covered the woman's death for whatever reason.'

The two men went their separate ways, one returning to the cottage to study the late woman's book, the other heading towards the island's only library. Though the building was stately, it was also rather dilapidated in places. Its roof was missing numerous tiles, whilst the door of the library was covered in scrapes. Barun entered the building to find that its front desk was unattended, and it took him several minutes of searching the aisles to locate a librarian. She was a rather snooty individual, and she rolled her eyes when Barun said that he wanted to see all the national newspapers over a three-month period in 1940. Barun was not entirely sure why she was so irritated by his request as the articles in question were already loaded into one of the microfilm readers. He thanked her regardless of her attitude, however, as Barun was not one to forget his manners.

Putting on his reading glasses, he began to scan through the newspapers. He was close to giving up when he found what he wanted. There she was, staring back at him. It was strange to think that the young woman who was smiling in the picture was the same person as the hideous spirit who had attempted to attack him the other night. The headline read: Tragic Bride Falls from Cliff on Her Wedding Day. A talented archaeologist, she had only moved to Corvid's Head a matter of months before she had died, and the story said that a man had been questioned about her death but was released without charge. Though the article was not short, it did give not give many details on the tragedy and hinted that it was death by misadventure.

Barun now had the date of the woman's death, her profession and, perhaps most importantly, he now had her name: Polly. Towards the end of the piece, there were a few interviews from local residents, and Barun almost leaped out of his chair when he read one of the names of those that had been quoted. Described as a young man who was about to become a deacon, a person by the name of Paul had told the reporter of how Polly had been a "remarkable" person and that her death was a loss to the whole island. Barun was confident that this was Father Paul, the same person whose name had come up sporadically during the investigation. He found a telephone and relayed the information that he had obtained to Sukhbir.

Once he had told him everything he had discovered, Barun gave a sigh. 'I still have concerns for Soumili's safety.

Perhaps you could go to try to convince her to leave the house, Sukhbir. I have already suggested that she finds somewhere else to stay, but she has this belief that her husband is going to come back to her.'

'Okay,' Sukhbir said. 'Where are you going?'

'It's about time Father Paul and I had a chat,' Barun said. 'Please take care when you visit that house, by the way. If you feel you are in danger, do not try to challenge this terror, as I fear it may be even more ferocious than we suspect.'

CHAPTER SEVEN

Dark clouds were gathering above Corvid's Head. It felt like the temperature had dropped by half a dozen degrees or more in the past hour, and Barun pulled the collar of his coat upwards to combat the chill. He had passed the church on many occasions, but this was the first time that was actually going inside it. Entering into a deathly silence, he immediately noticed a motionless figure stood in the nave. The priest did not turn to look at him at first, as it seemed as though he was so wrapped up in his thoughts that he did not notice that Barun was there.

'Father Paul,' Barun said, his voice bouncing off the stone walls.

The priest did not flinch at the sudden call of his name, and he slowly looked around. 'Yes?'

'My name is Barun Rai,' he said. 'I am assisting the police with their investigation into the deaths at the cliffs. It is my understanding that you visited the Banerjee's home recently.'

Father Paul lowered his head. 'I did, but there is nothing to talk about.'

'We both know that there is plenty to talk about. You encountered a spirit there, didn't you?'

Wincing as though he was in pain, Father Paul gave a dismissive gesture. 'There is no such thing as ghosts or—'

'Do not test my patience,' Barun interjected. 'If we don't act soon, Soumili, the woman who lives in that house, will likely die. I cannot stop this evil on my own; I need your help, Father.'

'And what can I do against such an awful power?' the priest asked, raising his own voice. 'I have already tried to banish it from the house and failed.'

'In truth, I do not know what can stop this thing, but I refuse to give up.' Barun took a few steps towards the priest. 'Many years ago, a woman called Polly died from falling from the cliffs. You two were close, weren't you?'

Father Paul turned his back on Barun. 'Close? In all honesty, Mister Rai, I loved her,' the priest said. 'The feeling, alas, was not reciprocated. She became engaged to Alexander, a rather horrid fellow. On the morning of their wedding, poor Polly discovered that he was still seeing a former girlfriend of his. Of course, Polly was heartbroken, but I knew her well, and never once have I believed that she took her own life. Did you know Alexander was questioned over her death? That was because an eyewitness saw them shouting near the cliff edge minutes before she fell. Of course, no charges were brought against him. Well, he left the island before the year was out. As the bible says: “the wicked flee”.’

‘What came of him?’ Barun asked.

‘I heard he died in Italy six or seven years later. Think he started mixing with a bad crowd.’

Father Paul shrugged. ‘At least he would have had to answer to his crimes in the next life.’

‘I hope you are right,’ Barun said. ‘Father, I read that Polly was an archaeologist. Did she have a knowledge of ancient rituals?’

‘Well, Polly was certainly well-travelled, and she could talk to you for hours about cultures that you had never even heard of before. So, to answer your question, I suppose she probably did know a fair amount about archaic practices and rituals. Why do you ask?’

Barun placed his hands in his pockets. ‘My associate and I discovered a notebook which belonged to her. In it, we found several passages written in old languages such as Aramaic. We are confident that before she died she placed a curse on all men on the island, a curse which also summoned a dreadful being into our world.’

The priest put his hand over his mouth for a moment as he contemplated what he had just been told. ‘People spoke of her dabbling in witchcraft, but I always thought that it was nothing more than gossip and hearsay.’ He wiped at his brow with a trembling hand. ‘When one finds themselves in a pit of despair, one can act in a reckless manner. I did not think she was capable of such a wicked deed, yet perhaps in her final hour on Earth she was blinded by hatred and unable to see the possible consequences of her actions.'

'I need your help stopping the evil that she brought forth,' Barun said. 'Polly made a terrible mistake, but she deserves to pass on to the other side. With your assistance, we might be able to free her soul.'

Father Paul grimaced. 'They are far too powerful. There is nothing we can do.'

'So you are prepared to let Soumili die and Polly remain as a thrall?' Barun asked, almost in a growl.

'I'm sorry, Mister Rai. I have nothing more to say on the matter.' Father Paul narrowed his eyes. 'If you don't mind, I need to organise tomorrow's service.'

Barun felt like grabbing the man by the shoulders, but he did not act on this impulse. Instead, he took out his notepad and began to write. 'This is the number for the cottage where I am staying. If you see sense, please phone me.'

Placing the scrap of paper on the pew nearest to the priest, Barun left the church. He started to walk in the direction of his lodgings but soon stopped dead in his tracks. When it came to facing paranormal threats, he was quite used to being underprepared, but on this occasion Barun was more than just unready: he did not have any idea at all of how he could defeat this horror.

*

Father Paul waited until the man had been gone for several minutes before picking up the note. He did not look at the piece of paper, simply slotting it at the front page of the bible he was holding. The church had been erected in the fifteenth century, not long after the War of the Roses. The architects of the time were wary of invasions, and they had built several sanctums and boltholes in the church to be used as hiding places during attacks. Centuries later, Father Damon had converted one of these rooms into his own personal study, and it was here that Father Paul found his mentor.

'You look like you are carrying the weight of the world on your shoulders,' Father Damon said when he looked up from the book he was reading.

'I have just had an interesting conversation with a gentleman who is investigating the recent falls,' Father Paul said. 'He is linking them to the entity that haunts the House on the Cliff.'

Father Paul proceeded to tell his mentor everything that Barun Rai had said to him. The old priest's expression did not change as he listened intently to Father Paul, though his wrinkled fingers did tighten around his walking stick when Polly's name was mentioned.

Once Father Paul had finished speaking, his mentor cleared his throat. 'I feel foolish that I did not see it before. This Barun Rai appears to be correct in his assessment,' Father Damon said, his voice markedly more husky than normal. 'Fetch that tome on the shelf there, friend. It has been some time since I have read it.'

Father Damon's loyalty to the church was absolute, though Father Paul did know of one occasion when his mentor had ignored the command of a cardinal. Five years ago, he had been ordered to destroy a certain book in his possession; the cardinal went as far as to claim that it was tantamount to sacrilege to store such an artefact within the grounds of a church. Father Damon had disobeyed. Never had he recounted the tale to any of his confidants of how such a respected priest such as himself had acquired a three-hundred-year-old book on the matter of demonology, nor had Father Paul ever dared to ask him. The book itself was always wrapped in a red, velvet cloth before it was put back in its usual spot on the bookshelf, and Father Paul pulled back this fabric away to unveil it. Whoever had written the book had been a disturbed individual. Graphic depictions of damnation were scrawled over its front cover, and Father Paul did not look at it for long before handing it to his mentor.

Father Damon placed it on the table in front of him and began to turn the book's fragile pages. The illustrations were not for the faint-hearted. On every other page there were vivid pictures of monstrous creatures that were beyond the stuff of nightmares.

'Ah. here it is.' Father Damon stopped on a page and pointed at a picture of a winged being. It had spindly legs like those of an emaciated mule and two mismatched eyes. 'We are dealing with a vengeance demon, a very deceitful one. It is called the Pervu Novak. Every time it takes a soul, it becomes more powerful. Polly is merely this thing's puppet, and it refuses to let her pass to the other side. If it adds another soul to its collection during the upcoming celestial event, there is no telling how formidable it could become.'

'Can it be stopped, though?' Father Paul asked.

Jutting out his jaw, Father Damon made a low, grumbling sound before he spoke. 'Are you certain that this man is in possession of a handwritten version of the curse?'

'That is what he told me.'

'Then there is a way,' Father Damon said, 'though it will be dangerous, and you will also need an assistant.'

*

Barun could hear the phone ringing through the door. Fumbling at his keys, he was able to run inside the cottage and pick up the receiver before the caller rang off.

'Hello?'

'It's Jenny.' Her voice was monotonous. 'There's been an incident at the station: Brian's escaped.'

Barun almost dropped the phone. 'Is anyone hurt?'

'He bit a chunk out of Constable Jenkins' ear,' Jenny said. 'He's in a bit of a mess and shook up, but he'll be alright. Strange thing was that Brian's cell door was unlocked when he jumped Jenkins whilst he was bringing him his dinner. I routinely check all the cell doors whenever I pass down that corridor, and I walked past that very door just ten minutes before the attack. I can't even begin to fathom how he got out.'

And we will never know how he did, Barun thought to himself. For a split second, he considered telling her where young Brian was going, yet he realised that he would only be putting Jenny and her colleagues in danger if she told her.

'I will keep an eye out,' he said.

'Thanks you, Barun. Unfortunately, we're only a small force so it might take us days to find him,' Jenny said. 'I'm going to have to have to go now, but you know where to find us if you see or hear anything.'

They ended the call, but the receiver was only down for a matter of seconds before the phone started to ring again.

'Is that you again, Jenny?' he asked after picking up the phone.

'No, it is Father Paul,' the priest replied in a solemn tone. 'Be at the house for seven o'clock tonight. Bring the book.'

The priest hung up the phone before he had given Barun a chance to reply.

*

Soumili's stomach grumbled. She had barely eaten or drank anything all day, and yet she did not feel hungry in the slightest. For most of the afternoon she had lain on her bed, occasionally craning her neck so that she could look at herself in the mirror. Soumili had turned her alarm clock to face the wall as she did not wish to keep track of the time that day. It was dark outside when she decided that she wanted to see Harmesh's face, so she pulled their wedding album from under the bed.

Every single picture brought back memories. Just as she was starting to feel as though going through the album was becoming too much to bear, she heard a voice which sent a tingle up her spine.

'Soumili,' a friendly, familiar voice called from downstairs.

Had she imagined it? No, it was too loud, too clear. She dashed from her room to the landing. It was almost exactly like the dream she had had, the one in which Harmesh had returned to her. Except there was one colossal difference: in her dream, it really had been her husband. The thing at the bottom of her stairs was not Harmesh. It had his looks. It had his smile. It even had his voice. But this was something imitating her husband. The Harmesh mimic was singing over and over again the chorus of the song that had played during the last dance of their wedding. Continuing to sing, it began to walk away from the bottom of the stairs in the direction of the kitchen.

'Wait, where are you going?' she called after him as she ran down the stairs.

She flicked the living room's light switch, but there came a popping sound as a light bulb blew out. Reaching for the switch of one of the table lamps, she pressed it to find that the blow out must have tripped the fuse box. In the gloom, Soumili crept into the kitchen.

'Harmesh?' she called out, her voice wavering.

They kept matches in the drawer nearest to the fridge, and despite the darkness Soumili was able to find the packet. She struck a match. The tiny light did not illuminate much, but she could now make out the silhouette of a man.

'Harmesh?' she asked again.

The person stepped forward, and Soumili screamed. It was Brian, the young man who had been caught trespassing on their property earlier in the week. There was something wrong with his eyes: they were milky-white. He cocked his head to one side then blew the match out.

*

Barun could have sworn that he had heard a scream. He knocked on the door once more, at the same time trying the handle. He had arrived at the House on the Cliff earlier than Father Paul for he had become worried about Sukhbir. His dear friend and colleague had not arrived back that afternoon at their lodgings, and the last contact Barun had had with him was when he had asked him to check on Soumili. Taking a step back from the door, Barun turned his attention to a nearby window. Pushing with all his might, he tried to force it open but his efforts were to no avail. He gave a disgruntled sigh. Barun could see now what he needed to do, though he did not like the idea of it one bit. Wrapping his coat around his arm, he smashed the window using his elbow.

Barun, once he had cleared away some of the broken glass, readied himself to clamber inside. Something bulky sprang at him from the darkness and connected with his face. Dazed, he staggered backwards onto the lawn. It took him a moment to figure out what had happened. The Banerjee's sofa had been dragged across the room by an unseen force, and it was currently pressed firmly up against the broken window. Barun placed his palms on the sofa then tried to push it away so that he could enter the house. It was hopeless. The spirits did not want him to get inside, and they were determined to block his way. Barun started to circle the house in an attempt to find an alternative means to gain entry to the building, though he found no realistic options other than breaking another window or scaling the rusty drainpipe. He was greatly relieved when he noticed that Father Paul was approaching him.

'Mister Rai,' the priest said. 'What's happened to your face? It's bleeding.'

'Don't worry about me.' Barun wildly gestured at the house. 'No one's answering the door, and I can't get in.'

'There's a cellar door over here.' Father Paul walked with purpose towards the house.

Wiping away a layer of dead leaves, the priest revealed a trapdoor which Barun had not noticed whilst he was surveying the building. The bolt was terribly rusted, but they were able to lift the door open. Father Paul led the way, Barun following closely after him. The light did not come on when they tried the switch, but fortunately Barun had brought his torch with him. After negotiating their way through the cellar, they ascended a staircase which led to the downstairs hallway. A crash sounded from the first floor, and Barun and the priest exchanged worried glances with one another.

Hotfooting it to the bedroom, they discovered that the noise had been the breaking of the room's window. Barun, deducing that the pane must have been smashed from the inside as there was very little glass upon the floor, was about to run over to see what had been thrown through it when he heard someone muttering. Father Paul identified where the voice was coming from before Barun, the priest's gaze drifting up to the ceiling. A floorboard in the attic creaked which confirmed that there was someone above them. Refraining from speaking, Barun nodded towards the loft hatch. As the two men drew closer to the latch, it became apparent that it was Soumili's muffled voice that they could hear.

Peculiarly, the ladder was nowhere to be seen, and Father Paul was required to fetch a chair so that they could climb up. There must have been nearly a hundred lit candles in the attic, and all the clutter in the room had been pushed to the sides. Though the weather outside was quite still, the rafters and the beams of the house were groaning terribly, a great pressure straining against the wood. Soumili was sat upon the floor rocking back and forth, and Barun moved to check on her. Father Paul's hand shot out and he grasped Barun's forearm to prevent him from approaching the woman.

'I would not advise getting too near to her, Mister Rai,' the priest whispered. Soumili snapped her neck back and started to laugh uncontrollably. Her eyes were a fiery orange, whilst there was a bluish tinge to her skin. Continuing to laugh, she writhed around on the floor as though she was a mere ragdoll being thrown around by an invisible hand. Father Paul was not distracted by the spirit's antics, and he set the contents of his bag upon a table.

'You have been present at exorcisms before, correct?' Father Paul asked.

'Yes.' Barun nodded.

'Good. I doubt you will have ever witnessed such a ferocious spirit, though the basic principles of the ritual itself still apply.' Father Paul kissed his bible before opening it. 'Do not look the demon in the eye, and certainly do not address it directly. I will signal to you when I require you to repeat a verse that I have just spoken aloud. You have the book?'

Barun pulled it from his pocket and held it aloft.

'Turn to the page on which the curse is written. When I am finished, I need you to pour this onto the ink.' Father Paul jabbed his forefinger in the direction of a vial upon the table. 'Once you have done that, one of us needs to say

Polly's name out loud which will, hopefully, draw the spirit from the body. Now, please can you make a circle around me, then we can begin.'

After Barun had drawn a circle around the priest using some chalk, the two men briefly shook hands and then Father Paul took up a position in front of the possessed woman.

'Pray to thee, our God, this day!' He raised his crucifix. 'I will set no vile thing before my eyes! I will have nothing to do with evil!'

Soumili's body thrashed around, and she pleaded for the priest to desist. This was a common trick used by malevolent spirits and demons, and one that fooled neither Barun or Father Paul.

'The power of Christ compels you!' Father Paul bellowed, waving at Barun with his free hand.

'The power of Christ compels you,' Barun repeated.

Soumili rose to her feet then gave the priest a mocking grin. 'This is my house.' The voice that came from Soumili's lips was not her own.

There came a crash above them, and dust particles fell from the rafters.

'He who speaks falsehoods,' Father Paul went on, 'won't be established before my eyes. Morning by morning. . . '

The being within Soumili started to taunt the priest by repeating his words back to him. 'Morning by morning!'

Suddenly, the sinister expression on her face turned to one of worry as her eyes reverted back to their correct colour. 'Barun, why are you doing this to me?' On this occasion, the voice that came from Soumili was indeed her own. 'Please save me. . . I'm scared.' She put her hands together, almost in a prayer.

'Soumili, is that you speaking?' Barun asked uncertainly.

The orange tint returned to her eyes, and she gave a cackle.

Father Paul continued with the ritual. 'I hate the deeds of faithless men. . . ' Calling out in agony, the priest dropped his crucifix to the floor.

Barun looked to the floor and saw the cause of the priest's cry: the metallic crucifix was glowing red with heat. Having branded the priest's palm, the demon laughed even harder. His brow furrowed in determination, Father Paul raised his bible with his uninjured hand.

'He who speaks falsehood won't be established before my eyes! Morning by morning…'

For the first time, it appeared as though the ritual was having its desired effect: Soumili's body started to curl up as the dreadful laughter stopped.

'I will have nothing to do with evil! He who speaks falsehood won't be established before my eyes! Won't be established before my eyes!' The priest was yelling at the top of his voice now.

Looking up to the ceiling, Soumili's body became still and the orange glow in her eyes dimmed. Barun knew that this meant Soumili was still in there, struggling against the spirit.

'Fight it, Soumili!' he called over the creaking of the house.

Father Paul paused whilst he studied the possessed woman. For a fleeting moment, it appeared as though the battle had been won, but then that terrible laughter came back. The demon inside Soumili looked to the two men, the burning in the woman's eyes brighter than ever.

'I will not leave her!' it shrieked.

Suddenly, a gust of air ripped through the attic. Barun, buffeted by the gust, would have been swept clean off his feet if he had not quickly taken a staggered stance. Once the blast had died down, it seemed as though it had resulted in nothing but a mere inconvenience to the men, but then Barun noticed that Father Paul had inadvertently touched the chalk circle with one of his heels. The demon did not hesitate. From Soumili's mouth poured hundreds of insect-like beings which flew at the priest before swarming around him. The creatures lifted him up off the floor, pinning him against the wall. Soumili's neck then twisted into an unnatural position, the demon turning its attention to Barun.

A set of icy-cold fingers wrapped around Barun's throat, and he was flung across the room. He landed on his shoulder, the pain so excruciating that he winced the moment he impacted with the floor. Despite the fact that the priest could barely move, Barun could hear that Father Paul was still carrying out the ritual. Just as he was pulling himself to his feet, Barun saw out of the corner of his eye that his foe was now by his side. The being within Soumili gave her body the strength of ten people, and it pushed Barun onto his back before it started to throttle him.

'May the holy cross be my light! Begone! Begone!' Father Paul called out. 'Barun, the diary! It's time!'

Though he heard his cue, Barun had neither the water nor the woman's diary in his possession. His eyes flitted to the table upon which he could see the faint glisten of the glass vial. The book, meanwhile, had at some point been knocked from the table, and it now lay open on the floor. There was no way that Barun could possibly overpower his assailant, but then an idea dawned on him. He kicked out at the leg of the table. On this first attempt, the sole of his shoe barely even brushed the leg, and the vial did nothing other than wobble ever-so-slightly. The phantom started to apply further pressure to Barun's throat causing his vision to become blurred. Knowing that he only had seconds before he passed out, Barun directed another kick at the table. This time he made a solid connection. There came the clink of glass. Instantly, the incredible strength left Soumili's body, and she withdrew her hands from Barun.

'Polly Anna,' Barun wheezed.

Flying backwards, Soumili landed on a chair. Another gust began to rage in the room; however, this one moved in the opposite direction to the previous flurry. A section of the roof fell in, moonlight flooding into the attic through the newly formed gap. Barun could do nothing but witness the carnage, and he pushed his back up against one of the walls.

'Take me now!' Father Paul called at the top of his voice. 'Let me be yours!'

Barun watched in horror as the winged creatures devoured Father Paul, the tattered remains of his clothing dropping to the floor without a morsel of flesh inside. As soon as they had killed the priest, the creatures themselves curled up and died before their bodies disintegrated into dust. The tempest around them grew into a whirlwind that began to swirl above Soumili's head. Furniture, boxes and many of the other objects within the attic were sucked towards the spiralling winds. Barun, meanwhile, was showered in a cloud of debris. Wiping dust from his face, he opened his eyes to see that the whirlwind was lifting Soumili's lifeless body out of the house. Leaping through the air, Barun knocked her out of the path of the whirlwind, latching onto her ankle and letting his body weight pull her down. There was silence. Barun looked around the room from his position on the floor. The winds had utterly subsided, and the only noise to be heard was the faint whirring of a police siren. Turning his attention to Soumili, he found that she was conscious with her eyes half-open.

'Over?' she asked in a weak mutter.

'Yes, it's all over,' Barun reassured her.

It took considerable effort for them to get out of the attic for they were both exhausted from the ordeal. As they were making their way out the house, Barun saw something which caused him to stop in his tracks. He had not seen the painting which was hung up in the hallway of the Banerjee's home before. It depicted a scene from a Greek tragedy, though it was not the subject matter that had caught Barun's attention. One of the figures in the background held a remarkable likeness to Brian, right down to the clothes he was wearing. The figure's mouth was open in a never-ending scream.

'What's the matter?' Soumili asked him in a hoarse voice.

'It's nothing Soumili,' he replied. 'It's nothing.'

The first person to approach them as they walked outside was Sukhbir. 'Is she okay?' Barun nodded to his friend. 'She will be.'

Walking with long strides, Inspector Jones was the next to head towards them. She gawped at them for a moment before taking Soumili by the arm and leading her away.

'I am sorry I wasn't there.' Sukhbir rubbed the back of his head. 'Someone jumped me while I was on my way here. They bound my hands and left me in a ditch. Lucky for me, the inspector noticed me when she was driving down that stretch of road.'

'Did you see the face of this person?'

Sukhbir's gaze drifted to the side. Barun, following his friend's gaze, saw the body of Brian upon the paving. Shattered glass was all around the body, whilst a pool of blood was seeping from under him.

'He obviously came out of the upstairs window, though a fall from that height shouldn't have killed him.' Sukhbir gestured.

'He didn't just fall.' Barun shook his head. 'I think he was thrown. Before Brian died, the spirit that was possessing him was transferred to Soumili, and it therefore no longer needed the poor man. I am of the belief that the spirit had picked Brian as a host because he was naive and therefore easier to manipulate than most.'

'And what exactly happened to the spirit?'

Barun took out his flask and had a swig; he had not realised just how thirsty he was until the moment the whiskey hit the back of his throat. 'It's gone. Where to, however, I cannot say.'

Epilogue

The sky was near cloudless, and the sun was beating down overheard. Placing his trowel down in the flowerbed, Father Damon wiped a bead of sweat off his forehead using the back of his hand. Whilst many of the flowers had begun to wilt already from the cooler weather, the rudbeckias he had planted last year were just starting to bloom. A shadow was cast over the flowerbed.

'Mister Rai, I was wondering when you would pay me a visit,' Father Damon said, languidly getting to his feet and turning to the man.

'That's remarkable,' Barun said. 'How did you know it was me just from my silhouette?'

'We are a small community.' Father Damon almost smiled. 'I could probably identify each and every person on the island from the sound of their footsteps, never mind their shadows.'

'Well, as you were already expecting me, you have probably already guessed what I want to talk to you about.' Barun's expression hardened. 'I was there in Father Paul's last moments.'

The priest made a motion with his hand, and the two men began to have a stroll in the church garden.

'I had guessed as much. Every day since I have regretted not going in his stead.' Father

Damon dropped his chin to his chest. 'I will rue it until the day I die.'

'You are being too hard on yourself. Father Paul knew the risks, and I do believe that he willingly sacrificed himself to free Polly's soul,' Barun said. 'He has likely saved the lives of hundreds.'

'Oh, I am well aware of all that. Nothing, however, will ever change my view,' Father Damon said. 'Anyway, enough about the regrets of an old man. How long are you planning on staying with us, Mister Rai?'

'I am catching the first ferry tomorrow,' Barun said. 'My colleague has already left to deliver a draft of our report to one of the universities we work for.'

'Hmm, a report,' the priest mumbled, pursing his lips. 'I would appreciate it if you left my name out of your work. My superiors do not take kindly to unauthorised exorcisms.'

'Consider it done.' Barun nodded. 'How do you plan to explain his death to them?'

'I am planning on going with whatever the police come up with,' Father Damon said.

'Somehow I cannot see spectres and ghouls being mentioned in their official report.' Barun stepped over a small picket fence that was in his path. 'A fair idea. Speaking of the police, should you need my assistance in the future, please contact Inspector Jones, and she will be able to put you in touch with me.'

'Thank you, Mister Rai, though I feel things will not come to that. As soon as the monster was expelled from the woman's body, it felt like a great gloom was lifted from the island. I believe for the first time in over thirty years, the members of our community can live without a sense of dread hanging over them. The cause of their woes has gone, and it is not coming back.'

Barun found it strange to hear such optimistic sentiments coming from a man wearing such a sullen expression. They stopped by the church gates.

'I do think you are right, Father.' Barun offered him a hand to shake. 'Maybe one day I will come back to visit.'

Father Damon stared at the hand for a moment before shaking it. 'You won't. People always say that, and they never do come back,' the priest said. 'I best go now as I'm expecting Brian Dawson's mother shortly for us to go over the funeral. Good luck on your future endeavours, Mister Rai.'

'Take care now.' Barun started to walk away before abruptly stopping. 'Oh, you will check in on Soumili from time to time, won't you? She has been through an awful lot.'

'Of course,' Father Damon said, his voice not quite as gruff as before. 'I don't tend to make house calls but for her I will certainly make an exception.'

Barun gave a stiff wave before leaving the church grounds.

He had been tempted to ask Father Damon for advice on the investigation that he was about to begin once he arrived back in mainland Britain, but Barun decided that it would have been unfair to ask for any more from him. Besides that, he reckoned there was a fair chance that even an experienced priest might not be able to help him with this one.

BARUN RAI AND THE COLONIST'S EXHIBIT

Belfast, Northern Ireland. 1968.

Their footsteps echoed as they made their way down a corridor that was situated deep within the bowels of the museum. Stopping at an ornate oak door, the security guard knocked three times. Barun and the guard waited in silence for a reply that did not come for several seconds.

'Come in,' a man from inside the room called in a brusque tone.

The guard who had escorted Barun to the office gave a timid gesture to the door before scuttling back to his post. Entering the room, Barun found a pale man with a thick moustache sat behind a sturdy desk.

'You must be the expert they've brought in,' the man said, placing his hands on his desk then leaning forwards. 'You deal a lot with this sort of thing?'

'I do, sir,' Barun said. 'I understand you're the curator?'

Picking up a glass of what appeared to be whiskey, the man examined it for a second before taking a sip. 'That I am. Arthur Brooke's my name. Been in charge here for almost twenty years now. I thought I'd seen it all until. . . I better just show you the place.'

Lethargically getting to his feet, the curator walked with a marked limp as he showed Barun the way to the exhibit. The lights within the glass cases were switched on, though the room's main lights were off giving the room an eerie atmosphere. On the opposite side of the room was the sarcophagus, the exhibition's main attraction. Despite being thousands of years old, the pharaoh's coffin was in remarkable condition and there were even traces of the original paint on its surface.

Barun noticed that the curator's gait and posture shifted somewhat once they had entered the room: the man walked at a slower pace with his head bowed and shoulders dropped.

'Well, here we are.' The curator gestured to his surroundings. 'I understand you have already been briefed?'

'That is correct,' Barun said. 'If you do not mind, I find I get better results when I am on my own.'

'Oh.' The curator looked down at his feet. 'I suppose that makes sense. The powers that be would not be happy if they found out that I left you here by yourself, so I would appreciate it if you could be discreet.'

Barun gave the man a thumbs up. 'Right you are.'

The curator left the room far quicker than he had entered it. Left to his own devices, Barun took off his coat and placed it on a nearby chair. He felt something brush against his shoulder blades, though he did not react to it.

At a leisurely pace, he started to make his way across the room with his hands behind his back, taking in the exhibits as he walked. The arrowheads and ceramic bowls did not interest Barun much; however, he soon came across an object that caused him to stop to admire it. Anubis was depicted in startling detail alongside Ammit the Devourer upon a solid gold bracelet that had small holes. Presumably they once held precious stones.

'That belongs to me,' a voice came from behind Barun.

In the reflection of the pristine glass, Barun saw a man's face. Weary, hooded eyes were glowering at him. Barun turned to look around the room and found no other sign of the spirit.

'Why are you looking away from me?' the spirit furiously asked.

Barun turned back to the case. 'Apologies, I was just wondering where you were.'

'I'm right here,' the spirit snapped.

'Yes, I realise that now,' Barun said calmly. 'You are Sir Theodore Hastings, correct?'

The spirit took a moment before he spoke. 'Who's asking?'

'I have been asked to convene with you as there have recently been some issues.' Barun placed his hands in his pocket. 'In the past few weeks, many people who have visited the museum have complained that you have disturbed them while they are trying to view the exhibit. I would like you to desist.'

The man's face wrinkled into a scowl. 'Would you now? Well, you can tell the people who stole my collection from me that I will be forthwith contacting the authorities. They are nothing but looters that have the gall to pass my possessions off as their own.'

'Can I ask you when was the last time you ate? Or perhaps the last time you slept?' Barun asked.

'If you are trying to ask me if I am aware that I am dead, then just spit it out, man!'

It was not the first time that Barun had come across a spirit that knew that they were no longer a member of the world of the living, though he was genuinely surprised that this abrupt, pompous man had been capable of establishing that he had breathed his last breath.

'So you already know that you are dead?'

'Of course I know. I'd had enough heart murmurs in my twilight years to know what the last big push would feel like,' the spirit replied, his tone slightly softer. 'The only matter that puzzles me is why I am still lingering here.'

'I do believe I can help you there.' Barun took one of his hands out of his pocket and pointed at the gold bracelet. 'That is just one of the hundreds of reasons why you have not passed to the other side. To leave this world, you must accept that they are no longer your possessions.'

After making a growling noise in the back of his throat, the spirit shook his head. 'I refuse. You know how much my collection cost me? Close to two-hundred thousand pounds. Why should I give it all away for nothing?'

'But all of these wonders once belonged to someone else, didn't they? They accepted that they could not take any luggage with them on their final journey. If you cannot do the same, you will spend eternity following these treasures around the world, both unhappy and restless forever.' Barun straightened himself. 'Move on, Sir Hastings. Be at peace now.'

The spirit's mouth grew thin, and he then gave a sharp nod. 'You make a good point. Thank you for your help, whoever you are.'

Gradually, the face in the glass faded away. Barun waited until the spirit had passed on to the other side before returning to the curator's office.

'Done already? I expected you to be at least an hour.' The curator rattled his fingers on his desk whilst studying Barun.

'Your problem has been solved,' Barun said. 'None of your customers who visit the exhibit will be bothered again.'

'Capital.' The curator clapped his hands together in jubilation. 'That is cause for celebration. Drink?'

Pouring himself a large whiskey, the curator signalled with his eyes to a second glass on his desk.

Barun raised his hand. 'No, thank you.'

'Suit yourself.' The curator placed his decanter down. 'You know, word had unfortunately got out about our little issue. It was when we noticed that our ticket sales last week were the worst of the year when we got in touch with your gaffer.'

'Gaffer?'

'Yes, gaffer. Your boss,' the curator said.

'Oh, I see. I never really considered the professor as my boss before.'

'Funny set-up you've got at that university.' The curator took a swig from his glass. 'Anyway, you've saved the museum a small fortune.'

'There's more to this life than money, Mister Brooke.'

Running his finger along his moustache, the curator looked at Barun as though he had just made an offensive remark about his appearance. 'Oh, is that right now? I think you'll find society as we know it would break down if we had a world without currency.'

'Perhaps, though that's not what I was getting at,' Barun said.

'And what are you getting at exactly?'

Barun opened his mouth to speak yet stopped. He had been awake for over twenty hours and did not feel like he had enough energy to have an argument. 'Never mind. I best be returning to my hotel.'

'Very well.' The curator leaned back in his chair and examined his glass. 'Good travels, Mister Rai.'

After giving the curator a respectful nod, Barun departed.

BARUN RAI IN THE DEN OF THE FOX

Lairg, Scotland. 1970.

A gale, ever-increasing in strength, swept across the moors. The thistles that spread to as far as the eye could see quivered in the wind. Wrapping his arms tighter to his chest, Barun concentrated on keeping himself on his own two feet. The taxi driver who had dropped him off in this desolate landscape had described the weather as "mild" for this time of year. If the locals considered this as fair conditions, Barun certainly did not want to pay a visit during the winter months. His only protection against the elements was the ancient sign at the crossroads, the post telling him that the nearest village was seventeen miles away. He checked his watch. They were late. Instinctively, he began to reach into his coat for a cigar before realising that smoking was probably not the best of pastimes to undertake given the adverse weather. The sun was beginning its descent, and within the next hour dusk would turn to night. On the horizon, a car appeared. Barun watched for several excruciating minutes as the car unhurriedly made its way along the road in his direction. When it came within twenty metres of him, his heart sank. It was not them. The driver of the maroon hatchback was an elderly woman with horn-rimmed glasses, and she stared curiously at Barun as she drove past him. And so he continued to wait. By the time his contact turned up, he had started to consider walking to a village to find a place to stay before it got dark. A battered off-road vehicle caked in mud pulled over, a grinning man in the passenger seat winding down his window to speak.

'If it isn't Barun Rai as I live and breathe.' The man beamed.

With his curly, golden hair and red cheeks, Sebastian Cooper would have looked like a renaissance painting of a cherub if it was not for his crooked nose. Some of the people who met Sebastian found his enthusiasm and positive outlook on life to be infectious. Everyone else found him downright irritating.

'Sebastian,' Barun called over the wind, as he approached the car. 'I was wondering if you were ever going to show.'

'My apologies for our lateness, old friend. Arthur here was refereeing a football match which went on longer than anticipated, and then after that our path got blocked by some escaped cattle.' Sebastian shrugged. 'You best get in before you catch a chill.'

Entering the car, Barun shuffled along the worn back passenger seats, the driver setting off the second he had shut the door. Their driver was a grizzled man wearing a flat cap, his amber eyes studying Barun through the rear view mirror.

'I'm Arthur,' the man said in a low tone.

'Pleased to meet you. I am Barun,' he said, giving a half-smile.

'Aye.' Arthur's eyes returned to the road.

'Arthur is the owner of the farm in question,' Sebastian said. 'We'll head there right away so that you can see what you think. I've already combed the place with my equipment, but I didn't come up with anything.'

Giving a snort, Arthur shook his head. 'I hope you do better than this lad, Barun. He's got some bleeding machine with an antenna that does nothing but bleep every five seconds.'

'As I have already explained, it measures electromagnetic fields,' Sebastian said with a sigh.

'All I know is that the only equipment I'll be carrying is on the back seat there.' Arthur jerked his thumb over his shoulder.

Barun turned to find that there was a shotgun in the boot, its barrel half-hidden by a blanket. 'Is that legal?'

'Course it's legal. Got a license and everything.' Arthur tutted. 'Had her since the war. Don't be touching her mind because she's got a hair trigger. Unlike you two, I've actually seen this beast for myself, and none of your fancy gizmos are going to do any good if it comes at you. That, on the other hand, will at least scare the blighter.'

'Well, I do not carry any *gizmos*,' Barun said calmly. 'Nor do I have any weapons on my person.'

Arthur stared at him again through the mirror. 'Aye, I can see you're travelling light. I thought you'd have a machine or something with you.'

'Sebastian and I are kindred spirits, but our techniques could not be more different. We were introduced following one my lectures at his college, and he has been trying to convince me that technology can match my own abilities ever since,' Barun said.

'And what are these abilities?' the old man asked.

Barun leaned forwards in his seat. 'It is probably better that I show you later rather than tell you now.'

'In truth, the lad hasn't said all that much about you,' Arthur said, furrowing his brow. 'All I know is that you're some kind of expert in strange goings-on.'

Barun had been called an expert in many things. Ghosts. The paranormal. Spooks. But strange goings-on was a new one to him.

'I refer to myself as a parapsychologist,' Barun said bluntly.

Arthur's grip on the steering wheel tightened ever-so-slightly. 'Right.'

The conversation came to an end, the old farmer seemingly unprepared to probe Barun as to what his occupation actually entailed. After several minutes of silence, Barun caught sight of an aura up ahead. He had not seen any spirits since encountering a foul-mouthed spectre that morning whilst he was waiting for his train to arrive. This lost soul was stood at the side of the road, its shoulders hunched and with a motorcycle helmet grasped in both hands. As they passed by them, there was a fleeting moment when the spirit realised that Barun could perceive them, their eyes meeting. They were in perpetual despair, lonely beyond mortal comprehension.

'Have there been any accidents on this road recently?' Barun asked when the spirit was no longer in sight.

'Aye, a poor lad came off his bike last year,' Arthur said in a quiet voice. 'Terrible it was. I've known his mother for nigh on forty years. At least he's at peace now, I suppose.'

Barun could not bring himself to tell the man that he was actually incorrect.

*

With its ramshackle roof and crooked chimney, the farmer's home looked as though it would fall in on itself from a gentle breeze. Barun was not sure what he had been expecting, but he had certainly not anticipated something so dilapidated.

'Here we are, lads,' Arthur said, parking the car next to a nearby shed. 'Though the place admittedly ain't much to look at, the walls don't half hold the heat in well during the winter. Normally I'd invite you in for a quick dram, but I can see we're losing light by the second.'

'Yes, it is probably best we press ahead,' Barun said. 'Please can you show me where the incident took place.'

Investigating unexplained livestock deaths was an unusual job, even for Barun. An entire flock had been savaged in a single night, which though was remarkable in its own right, it was not the reason that had enticed him to travel hundreds of miles north from his temporary lodgings in Birmingham. When Sebastian had contacted him, he had spoken of a poacher who had witnessed the incident. The miscreant had been so shaken from what he had seen that he handed himself into the police and demanded that they lock him in a cell. He had described a shadow silently picking off the flock one by one before stealing into the night. Needless to say, there had been only a handful of people that had believed his account.

The old farmer led them over a stile and into a paddock. Immediately, Barun began to sense the echoes that the being had left behind. He lowered his eyelids. It had moved at great speeds. There were signs of method in its attacks, slaying the strongest members of the flock first before dealing with the smallest. It had possessed the animals and stopped their hearts. This spirit was unlike anything Barun had ever come across. It was not malevolent and certainly had not taken pleasure in killing. To this entity, the whole act had been based on instinct. For some reason that Barun could not fathom, his visions were fragmented as though some unseen force was trying to conceal from him what had happened.

Opening his eyes, Barun found that the two men were staring at him.

Sebastian gave a weak smile. 'You know what happened, don't you?'

‘Not quite.’ With his energy sapped, Barun stumbled over to a fence so that he could lean against it. ‘I have seen flashes of the incident, but not enough to explain why the attacks happened or if there could be a repeat.’

‘A repeat?’ Arthur asked, scowling. ‘I lost hundreds of pounds in a single night. If this was to happen again, I’d be ruined.’

‘Relax, he isn’t saying he can’t stop it,’ Sebastian said. ‘Are you, Barun?’

He did not answer, his attention drawn to the fence post upon which his hand was resting. Carved into it was a crude symbol.

‘What is this marking?’ he asked them.

‘Oh, that,’ Arthur said, walking over to join him. ‘My grandfather etched that over a hundred years ago. All the posts other than the new ones have them on.’

Barun raised an eyebrow. ‘New ones?’

‘Yes, there was a storm a couple of weeks back. Posts were ripped clean out of the ground.’ He gestured to his right. ‘Only a minor upset compared to losing an entire flock, of course.’

Barun studied the area. Even though it was such a great distance away from Barun, the new fencing was a stark contrast to the rest of the enclosure. Behind this section of the fence was a wood upon an embankment. He quickly turned back to the symbol, taking off his gloves so that he could run a finger over it. The mark consisted of eight intersecting lines giving it an appearance similar to that of a snowflake, and around this symbol had been carved tiny runes at the end of each of its lines.

Barun snapped his fingers. 'Of course,' he muttered to himself.

'What is it?' Arthur asked impatiently.

'I am no expert in ancient languages, but I do believe this is Old Nordic,' Barun said, pulling his gloves back on. 'The shapes and patterns suggest to me that your grandfather put these runes here to ward off spirits. Once the fence was replaced, there was no deterrent in place to keep the being away from your flock. You said before that you have seen it, Arthur. Pray tell me where this was?'

Arthur took off his cap and scratched at his scalp with his grubby fingernails. 'As it happens, I saw it in the woods while my handyman and I were putting up the fence.'

Subconsciously, Barun started to slowly wander towards the woodland. 'And what did it look like?'

'I can't recall too much about it in all honesty.' Arthur puffed out his cheeks. 'It was a great beast with red fur, the like of which I have never before seen. All I fully remember were its eyes. They were like two sapphires they were. When I was a child I was told not to stray too deeply into the woods, and now I know why.'

Barun wiped at his face as he racked his mind. 'Your account of this creature has left me at a loss. I was starting to formulate a theory that centred around it being a spirit, not an entity of flesh and bone.'

'Sorry to butt in, but I've just had a thought,' Sebastian piped up. 'Surely all we need to do is carve the same symbols onto the other posts, and it'll stay away for good.'

'If only it was that straightforward.' Barun stopped in his tracks and looked back to the men. 'One cannot simply duplicate the pattern, as an incantation must be spoken aloud whilst the runes are being etched. Without an incantation, the runes would hold no power.'

'Sort of like a blessing then?' Arthur asked.

'If you like.' Barun shrugged.

Arthur placed his cap firmly back on his head. 'So, Mr. Rai, if I cannot keep this monstrosity at bay, what do you suggest I do? Move home? Or bring in a shaman to perform this ritual?'

'I do not suggest that you do anything at present,' Barun said calmly. 'Even if we were to find a person capable of speaking the appropriate incantations, this being would still remain a threat to future generations. It has therefore become apparent to me that I must confront this spectre, and I intend to do this alone.'

Sebastian gawped. 'We can't let you do that, Barun. You aren't even entirely sure of what this thing is.'

'And that is the exact reason why I must do this by myself,' Barun said.

'I'm going.' Sebastian put his hands on his hips.

From the expression on the man's face, Barun knew that there was no chance that he could convince him to change his mind.

'So be it.' Barun let out an audible sigh. 'But I will only have company on one condition: if you are to come with me, you mustn't bring any weapons with you. One thing I do know is that it is capable of possessing the living, and should it take control of a person whilst they were holding a knife or a gun. . . well, I don't need to explain what could happen.'

'No way I'm going in there without my gun,' Arthur grumbled. 'If you two had seen what I'd seen, you wouldn't go anywhere near those trees without being armed to the teeth. If you want to risk your necks, it's your funeral.'

'Maybe you are right, and I'm being naive, but my gut instinct tells me that I must stick to my morals.' Barun took his notepad from his pocket then started writing. 'Should we not return, please can you contact this man and tell him what happened. Under no circumstances should anyone go into the woods looking for us. Is that understood?'

Arthur, a man quite clearly unaccustomed to receiving orders, took the scrap of paper and stared at it with wide eyes as he struggled to find a response. 'Aye. . . I can do that.'

'Good man.' Barun clapped his hands together. 'Right, if there is nothing else to discuss, we best be on our way.'

Having picked up a torch each from the boot of Arthur's car, Barun and Sebastian began to head for the trees. Sebastian brought with him a handheld device that measured the temperature. Though it was well accepted in the field of paranormal research that reading the temperature for any sudden drops could help to indicate if spirits were nearby, Barun was unsure how effective this method would prove to be in an already cold climate. Given their current situation, however, he did not feel it was appropriate to question Sebastian over his logic despite these doubts.

The ferocity of the wind had diminished slightly in the past half hour, yet it remained strong enough to make the branches overhead creak and groan. There was a peculiar stench in the air that was not befitting of woodland, a smell reminiscent of rotting food.

'What is that?' Sebastian asked in a quiet voice, as he sniffed at the air.

'No idea, but I do believe we should follow our noses,' Barun said.

The slope that the wood was situated on suddenly became much steeper for a short distance until the land levelled off entirely. It was in this place where the light from their torches revealed the first of the grisly discoveries. Bird carcasses were strewn across the ground, maggots and flies feasting upon the carrion. Despite the decay around them, Barun noticed that the smell here was fresh and fragrant, as though they had just walked into a field of flowers.

'I take it you're getting that? It's remarkable,' Sebastian said in a child-like amazement. 'I've read dozens of research papers about phantom odours, but none of them did justice to actually experiencing them in real life.'

Unlike his companion, Barun was greatly concerned by the change of scents. 'A foul smell to deter us from going further, then a sweet one to entice us. This is a clever spirit that is trying to perplex us.'

'I have heard before of poltergeists being capable of creating a variety of. . . ' Sebastian trailed off.

Ahead of them was a small clearing where, upon a slab in its centre, there was a dead animal. Cautiously, they approached. A deceased fox lay upon the stone, and unlike the carcasses they had passed on their way to the clearing, there were no visible signs that it had start to decompose. Its tongue lolled out from its jaws, whilst its legs were straight and rigid. Barun shone his torch down at the animal for a while and pondered. Suddenly, it all made sense to him.

'This is the creature that the farmer saw,' Barun said dreamily.

Sebastian stared at him incredulously. 'That sorry-looking thing? Arthur talked about a beast; I hardly think a farmer of his experience and age would be scared of a common fox.'

'When the old man laid eyes upon this creature, it was likely far bigger,' Barun explained. 'During my spell studying in Nepal, I met a Japanese priest who told me in length about trickster spirits in his homeland. He called them Kitsune. They could inhabit any other living creature that they so liked through means of possession, though their natural form was a spectral fox. Another of their abilities is that they can even change the appearance of whatever they possess.'

Sebastian nodded to himself. 'So that would explain what Arthur saw. But why would something clearly so forceful use its power to kill livestock? Is it primitive?'

'Not at all, this creature is both methodical and intelligent. In comparison, spirits of late humans tend to not know that they are no longer a member of the world of the living, and on the occasions they do attack, they are often indiscriminate.' Barun crouched down to inspect the body further. 'My visions on the field were also disrupted by an unknown force, something that wanted to hide its tracks. This was surely the spirit trying to stop us from locating it, which means it must either be afraid of the living or wish to conceal a motive from us.'

'Fascinating.' Sebastian also squatted down. 'If it is this Kitsune like you say, I suppose it would make sense for it to take possession of the one creature on earth that most resembled itself. I wonder if this animal died of old age or–'

Barun was too slow to react; Sebastian's hand had reached out to touch the animal before Barun had even had a chance to let out a panicked cry to warn the man. There was a blinding light, and Barun was knocked onto his back. A noise like a thousand glass bottles being smashed simultaneously sounded, as the light began to dim. Still dazed, Barun sat upright. Sebastian's lifeless frame was floating in mid-air above the slab. By the man's feet was sat the fox, its blue eyes staring intently at Barun.

'I have been listening to your words,' the creature said in a gravelly voice, though its mouth did not move at all. 'Tell me, are you a shaman?'

Calmly, Barun took to his feet. 'I am not, though this is not the first time I have been confused for one.'

'I see,' the spirit said. 'Then explain why you have sought me out.'

Barun now noticed that his hand was stinging and discovered that he had suffered an injury when he had fallen, blood flowing from his palm. 'I will once I know what you have done to my friend.'

The fox languidly turned to look up at Sebastian. 'He is between your world and mine. When I understand the purpose of your intrusion, I may release him if I am satisfied.'

Taking a handkerchief from his pocket, he placed down his torch and began to bandage his hand. 'Very well. My name is Barun Rai. The farmer who owns the lands to the south tasked my friend and I with identifying what killed his livestock. After surveying the scene, I followed a trail which ended here. I believe it was you who was behind the deaths, yes?'

'It was I,' the creature said. 'A century ago, I made a deal with the shepherd who lived in that building. I was to protect his sheep from harm, and in return he would make offerings to me. Then, one winter, I received nothing. When I ventured out to confront the shepherd, I found that runes, ones not of my tongue, had been placed around the fields to stop me from entering his lands. I was infuriated by this slight.'

'And the recent storm disposed of part of the barrier, so you took your opportunity to take revenge.' Barun narrowed his eyes. 'Did you ever consider that the man may have died, and this was why the offerings stopped?'

'If that is the case, then he should have told his offspring of our deal so that they could have continued to pay respects in his stead. No, there are no excuses for his insult.' The creature stirred. 'Now, I have listened to you long enough, and I am unimpressed. Whether you have entered my domain as a peacemaker or to vanquish me, I care not. You will not be leaving here alive, *Barun*.'

There came a crunch of a twig snapping underfoot. Barun fumbled at his torch and turned the beam towards the trees. A dead man, his body rotten to the bone, was shambling in his direction. Barun heard another noise and saw that the spectre was not alone. Scanning the torch in a full circle, he discovered that he was utterly surrounded.

'You do not need to bring these poor souls into a matter between us. Call them off,' Barun demanded.

'No,' the spirit intoned. 'Millennia ago, the humans in these lands would appease me by sacrificing their own kind on this very rock. Now those that were sacrificed are my servants, and soon you will be joining their number.'

Barun felt his heart rate grow faster as the spectres crept ever closer to him. Slowly breathing out through his nose in an attempt to calm himself, he cast his mind back to the conversation he had had with the priest regarding the Kitsune. He recalled the man telling him that they were vulnerable to iron whilst in their true form, but even if he could convince it to be drawn away from the creature it was presently inhabiting, Barun had no way to harm it. The spectres were a matter of metres away from him now, their pale eyes trained on him. He closed his eyes tightly and tried the best he could to ignore his current predicament. Suddenly, it came to him, the memory hitting him like a slap across the face.

Opening his eyes, he stared at the Kitsune. 'I must warn you, the farmer said that if my friend and I were not return to him by dawn, he planned to comb this wood with a party of hunting dogs to drive you out,' Barun said.

The spectres came to a complete standstill.

'The man owns dogs?' the spirit asked, a hint of unease in its tone.

'Yes, he has a kennel but a mile away where he keeps all twenty of them.' Barun straightened himself up to his full height. 'He told me he wasn't going to feed them in the morning.'

Barun studied the fox and noticed one of its paws was quivering.

The creature blinked. 'How do I know you are telling the truth?'

'You don't, but are you willing to take that risk?' Clearing his throat, Barun took a step forwards. 'If you were to let us go though, not only would I stop him from letting the beasts loose, I would also see to it that the farmer resume the agreement that was made between yourself and his ancestor.'

'What would he bring me?' it asked curiously.

'There is ample game in this region. I am confident he could bring you plenty of meat,' Barun said. 'Would that suffice?'

'What about whiskey? His forefather would leave me whiskey in a dish, and I acquired a taste for it after a while.' The creature licked its lower lip.

'I am certain that could be arranged.' Barun smiled.

'Very well. In the morning, I expect to find an offering at the border of my domain,' the creature said. 'Be warned, should I not be satisfied with what has been left, my servants shall lay waste to these lands.'

'I understand.' Barun gave a respectful nod.

Out of the corner of his eye, he perceived that the spectres were shrinking away. The Kitsune, however, did not depart. After several seconds of motionlessness, the creature that was under its possession started to violently convulse. Its muscles bulged unnaturally, as it increased in size. Just as it looked as though the fox's skin was about to tear from the pressure, the creature began to wretch before spitting something from its jaws. Barun watched in surprise as the oddity that had emerged from the beast's mouth began to unfurl. A small, hairless being with pointed ears staggered onto the stone slab, its four spindly legs trembling with every step it took. Meanwhile, the bloated body of the fox started to decay at a remarkable speed, and within moments all that was left of the animal were its bones.

Barun had once viewed a tapestry depicting a Kitsune in an exhibition. Peasants and nobles alike had been portrayed as watching in marvel at the beauty and majesty of the snow-white Kitsune, with its strong neck and seven tails, as it flew over their heads. Its elegance had been practically regal, and Barun recalled that the artist had given the spirit a human-like expression of pride. The wretched being before him now was the antithesis of what had been depicted in the tapestry. For one thing, it was more reminiscent of a newborn rabbit than a fox, its skin pink and wrinkled; furthermore, it also had just three tails which each dragged along the ground like pieces of string. Sebastian, who had remained unconscious throughout the ordeal, fell to the ground with a thud.

'Leave here with this friend of yours.' The Kitsune's real voice was shrill, almost unbearably so. 'Should I ever see you again, Barun Rai, I will not hesitate to extinguish your life.'

*

Embers fluttered up the chimney, as the firewood gently crackled. The glow from the flames was the only source of light in the living room, whilst there was a draught coming from the window frame which caused the curtains to rustle. Arthur tottered over to the fireplace and gave it a jab with his poker. Picking a hot water bottle off the floor and holding it to his chest, Barun winced as the heat met his bruised ribs.

'You alright there, good man?' Arthur asked, returning the poker to its stand.

'Just a bit tender,' Barun replied.

'Not surprising.' Arthur sat down in the armchair opposite to his guest. 'Can't believe you carried the lad all that way back with you.'

'It was not the journey back that was the problem,' Barun said.

The two men sat in silence for a moment, as Arthur poured himself a drink.

'The lad's out for the count next door on a camp bed,' Arthur said. 'Can't see him being awake before midday.'

'He'll need plenty of rest over the comings weeks. There are very few people on this planet today who have spent as long as he has within the corridor that lies between life and death.' Barun leaned over to pick up his mug from the nearby coffee table.

'I deeply regret not going with you having heard what happened.' Arthur shook his head.

'You have nothing to regret. No good would have come from all three of us being put through such an ordeal,' Barun said softly. 'Of course, you now have your own task anyway: making an offering.'

'Oh yes, pheasants and whiskey. At least this thing has good tastes.' Arthur took a sip from his drink. 'To think this fiend has been there for all this time. And why did my grandfather never tell anyone of this deal he made with it? That's something I still can't get my head around.'

'He may have intended to tell someone before he died yet put it off until it was too late, possibly because he feared ridicule,' Barun said. 'If you had not seen the creature for yourself, I doubt that you would have believed my account.'

Arthur scratched at his chin. 'My grandfather was a very proud man, so you may have a point there. That still can't stop me from wishing that he'd said something. If he had, perhaps we could've found a way to scare it off.'

'Even if we were able to assemble the greatest exorcists and mystics in the world, I am uncertain whether you would have enough strength to expel it from the land it has claimed as its own,' Barun said. 'You should look on the Kitsune as a force of nature, a power that can be contained, yet not destroyed.'

Arthur raised an eyebrow. 'So I'm living on the doorstep of a volcano?'

'I perhaps would not put it so dramatically.' Barun gave a half-smile.

'Oh well, I guess all's well that ends well.' After raising his glass, Arthur sank his drink.

Staring vacantly into the fireplace, Barun's smile gradually faded. All was not well. Not in the slightest. If he had never learned of the Kitsune's greatest fear, his soul would have been condemned to wander that wood until the end of time itself. There would certainly come a day – maybe not for many years – when an unfortunate individual would unwittingly stumble into its lair, and there was nothing Barun could do to prevent this from occurring. He was so wrapped up in his train of thought that he did not catch the farmer's next question.

'Sorry, what did you say?'

'I asked if there was anything else I could do,' Arthur said.

'Oh. . . right. Well, I may have been tempted to seek out a person capable of crafting runes to restore the barrier between the Kitsune and your pasture, but the spirit made clear that it was angered that your grandfather had placed warding runes there in the first place.' After taking a sip from his drink, Barun put the mug back on the table. 'However, there is something I strongly recommend.'

'And what's that?'

'Get a dog.' Barun folded his arms. 'In fact, I advise getting several.'

BARUN RAI AND THE SHRIEKING CUPBOARD

Colombo, Sri Lanka. 1972.

Her trembling hand caused the cup she was holding to rattle against her saucer. The woman's gaze, meanwhile, bore into the ground by Barun's feet. With his hands behind his back, her husband, seemingly absent-mindedly, was tapping one of his feet repeatedly on a particularly creaky floorboard.

'Are you positive you still want to go ahead with this, Anaya?' Rihaan asked his wife.

Anaya blinked. 'Yes. I just need a minute.' She took a sip of her camomile tea.

'Please do not rush yourself,' Barun said. 'I appreciate that this must be difficult for you.'

Rihaan walked behind his wife's chair and placed a comforting hand on her shoulder.

Clearing her throat, Anaya rested her cup and saucer on her thigh. 'Have you ever come across something that you are unable to comprehend, Mister Rai?'

'There have indeed been occasions in which I have seen something that has left me perplexed.' Barun entwined his fingers.

'Good. Hopefully, there is then a chance that you will believe at least some of what I am about to tell you.' Anaya briefly touched her husband's hand before returning it to her lap. 'Last year, Rihaan's niece came to stay with us for a while. She went off to work in Hong Kong a couple of months back, and all these issues seemed to start as soon as she went. It was small things at first like paintings falling off walls and doors slamming in the middle of the night. Then it suddenly got much worse. One night, at a quarter past eleven, I was sewing at the kitchen table when I heard three booming knocks. I went upstairs to investigate, though I found no sign of whatever caused the noise. Then it happened at exactly the same time the night after. And then the night after that. It took me two weeks to locate where the noise was coming from. We have a cupboard in our guest room that has been in my family for generations. I waited outside the room one night and saw it rock back and forth like there was someone inside it thrashing around. My husband has a couple of pistols, and I'd made sure to bring one of them with me. So I ran to the cupboard with a gun in hand and threw the door open. There was nothing in there other than an old coat of mine on a hanger. It took me a while to convince Rihaan that I hadn't lost my mind. He saw it move himself one night, and he moved it to the cellar the next morning with help from our neighbour.'

Barun looked at Rihaan then back to his wife. 'That is indeed mysterious. May I ask: why did you not simply dispose of the cupboard?' Barun asked.

'Rihaan suggested that only it's been in my family for so long.' Anaya's eyes welled-up as she spoke. 'Is there anything you can do, Mister Rai?'

'I'm sorry for being so non-committal, though at this time I can neither say yes nor no. What I can do is promise you that I will do everything in my power to get to the bottom of this,' Barun said. 'I'm presuming that none of your family have ever told you of any strange stories involving the cupboard?'

'None at all.' Anaya dabbed at her eyes with her knuckle. 'That's what makes this all the more peculiar. I do wonder if it's my grandmother, yet why would she suddenly return to me over thirty years after her death?'

'There is a chance it could be her. Spirits have been known to lie dormant for years before making themselves noticed. Perhaps she is trying to warn you of a future event,' Barun said. 'Do you have anything you want to add, Rihaan?'

The man looked genuinely surprised by the question. 'I do not think so.'

'Very well.' Barun stood up then looked at his watch. 'I've got five to eleven meaning I haven't got much time. Can I please be shown to the cellar?'

'Of course. Follow me,' Rihaan said.

Upon leaving the living room, the two men passed through a bead curtain into the kitchen. A chair was propped up against the small door which led to the cellar.

'There's no light down there,' Rihaan said, moving the chair to one side. 'I hope you're alright with a lantern.'

'No problem at all.' Barun smiled. 'My work has taken me deep into mines and caves before, so I can assure you that I'm well used to the dark.'

Rihaan lit a kerosene lamp and handed it over to Barun. The moment the door was opened, they were hit with a musky smell that offended the nostrils. Barun wafted at the dust particles that had escaped the cellar with his spare hand before peering down the wooden steps.

'If you hear any shouting or loud noises, please do not come to check on me.' Barun raised his lamp a little so that he could see further down the steps.

'Are you expecting there to be any risks involved?' Rihaan asked.

'I cannot be sure what is inside this cupboard of yours.' Barun shrugged. 'For that reason, I am simply preparing for every eventuality. Wish me luck.'

Rihaan waited until Barun had completed his descent before closing the door. His eyes took a moment to adjust to the near darkness. A tiny crack of light from the gap beneath the door penetrated the room, but other than that there was no other light except for Barun's lantern. There was a whistling noise coming from somewhere in the darkness which Barun guessed was the wind running through the house. Barun lifted his lamp and caught sight of it. He was unsure how Rihaan and his neighbour had been able to get such a bulky piece of furniture down the narrow steps, but there the cupboard was, sat in the middle of the room. At first glance, there was nothing unusual about the cupboard's appearance, though Barun sensed that there was something greatly amiss. He checked his watch to find that he still had ten minutes to go. Taking his flask from his coat pocket, he had a swig from it before he started to inspect the cupboard. Firstly, he opened its doors and peered inside. In his experience, cursed items occasionally had inscriptions etched into them, yet Barun could find no signs of any engravings. With time quickly running out, Barun placed his palm on the cupboard then closed his eyes. Though he did not hear the voices of any spirits, he did feel a great sorrow come over him, the emotion so strong that it felt as though he was attending the funeral of one of the members of his family. He withdrew his hand and once more looked at his watch. Ten past eleven. Out of ideas, Barun pulled up a box and, after placing it in front of the open cupboard doors, he sat down on it. Barun began to stare into the blackness as he waited. Finally, he heard three loud noises. Anaya had described the sounds that came from the cupboard as "knocks" yet it was not the word that Barun would have used. To him, they sounded like three blasts.

A figure materialised within the cupboard. Though they were shrouded in darkness, Barun could make out that they were a slender woman wearing a pale blue dress. The spirit took a step out of the cupboard and into the light of Barun's lantern. She had a yawning wound in her neck from which ran a thin stream of blood, and her hair was matted. Intrigued by Barun, she cocked her head to one side and took a half-step towards him. Now that he could see her more clearly, Barun identified two more wounds that the poor woman had sustained in the final moments of her life. All three wounds were unmistakably gunshot wounds.

'My name is Barun,' he said confidently. 'Do you want to talk to me?'

The spirit grabbed at her own hair with both hands and started to wail.

Barun stood up. 'I might be able to help you.'

Abruptly, the spirit ceased crying then clenched her teeth together. She turned to Barun and let out a snarl.

*

The clock in the lounge struck a quarter to twelve just as Barun entered the room. It appeared as though Anaya had barely moved a muscle since Barun had last seen her, whilst her husband was leaning against the mantelpiece.

Anaya leaned forwards in her chair. 'Did you find anything?'

'I did.' Barun noticed his hands were dusty and rubbed them on his coat.

'Well?' Rihaan asked, lowering his eyebrows.

'Anaya, if you wouldn't mind, I would like to speak to your husband alone,' Barun said.

Letting out a nervous laugh, Anaya looked to her husband then quickly back to Barun. 'I do not follow,' she said. 'What have you have discovered down there?'

'Just please do as he says.' Rihaan looked down at his shoes. 'Go next door and sit with Mayra. She will appreciate your company.'

Anaya opened her mouth as if to speak, but she then pressed her lips together and left the room without saying another word. Barun stayed standing by the door for he was not sure how Rihaan would react; therefore, he did not want to potentially present the man with an opportunity to corner him by walking away from the only exit.

'So? What did you find?' Rihaan asked.

'You already know what I found. Why did you kill her? Why did you kill your niece?' Barun asked.

At first, the man stared at Barun as though he was waiting for a punch line to a joke, but then he put his head in his hands and groaned. 'I called you here to put my wife's mind at ease. I reckoned you would just be some con artist medium waving tarot cards around. If I had known you were actually the real thing, I would never have brought you into my home.'

'Are you going to answer my question? Why did you do it?'

'Because she was trying to blackmail me. I made a business deal in my younger days that was not exactly legitimate, and she told me she would go to the police unless I gave her a small fortune.' Rihaan placed his hands in his pockets. 'I think many men would have done what I did if someone was trying to extort money from them.'

'No, I for one think there are very few people in this world that would ever resort to murder,' Barun said.

Rihaan narrowed his eyes and looked Barun up and down. 'So you would have paid her?'

'In your position, I would have gone to the police and confessed to my crimes.' Barun shrugged.

'That was a stupid question, wasn't it? A man like you would never find yourself in my situation. You're a real upright citizen. I bet if you found a coin on the ground, you'd try to find who dropped it.' Rihaan suddenly took his hands out of his pockets and clapped them together. 'Enough of all that. What did you find in my cellar? Is she gone for good this time?'

'Yes, she is at rest now.' Barun stared vacantly into the fireplace. 'She had appeared to me not long a quarter past eleven, the time she died. Unfortunately, we did not share a common language, and she spoke to me in Tamil. I know the odd word or two and was able to figure out who she was, though how she had actually died was something I had to ascertain for myself.' Barun made his hand into a gun and pointed at Rihaan. 'You shot her three times with a pistol from close range. Wrongly, you believed she was dead whilst you put her body in a sack. You must've been interrupted because you then threw her body into the cupboard, and it was in here that she passed away.'

A sinister smile spread across Rihaan's face. 'Very good, Mister Rai. I must ask you how were you able to deduce all this?'

'There was no blood within the cupboard; therefore, she must have been stored or wrapped within something. Secondly, you come across as a very methodical man, so the idea of you bundling a body into your wife's favourite piece of furniture didn't make any sense to me,' Barun said. 'My gut feeling is that it was your wife who returned home earlier than expected, and you were forced to make changes to your plans. As for the method you used to kill her, I saw the bullet wounds with my own eyes, and Anaya also mentioned that you own pistols. In other words, it was entirely clear that you shot her.'

'You are very close, Mister Rai, though it was in fact our housekeeper who entered unexpectedly.' Rihaan leisurely walked over to a bureau and picked up a pear from the fruit bowl upon it. 'So what happens now?' He wiped the pear against his jacket.

'What happens now is entirely up to you. One option is that you dispose of me in a similar fashion to how you got rid of your niece.' Barun folded his arms. 'But you are not going to do that.'

'Oh, and why's that?' Rihaan asked before taking a bit of his pear.

'Because that in actuality poses a higher risk than letting me go. I am not in possession of the murder weapon nor do I know where the body is,' Barun said. 'Also, though you touched on your motive, you were clever enough to not give me many details. I am, of course, not a citizen of Sri Lanka, and so if I went to the police, who are they going to believe? A respected businessman like yourself or a foreigner who is without a shred solid evidence?'

Rihaan wiped his mouth with the back of his hand. 'You are a clever man, Mister Rai. If we had not met in these circumstances, I am sure we would have got on very well together.'

'Perhaps you are right. Now, you called me here to cleanse your home of a spirit, and that is what I have done. Whether you hand yourself into the police or not is no concern of mine.' Barun turned to leave. 'I've got a plane to catch early in the morning, so if you don't mind I will take my leave.'

'Goodbye, Mister Rai. I do hope you don't do anything foolish such as telling anyone about our little conversation,' Rihaan said.

Barun did not respond, instead giving something reminiscent of a wave before leaving. The neighbourhood of Colombo that he was in was one of the more affluent areas, and he had to pass through an iron gate to leave the grounds of the house. Barun's next destination was an abandoned textiles factory three streets away. Before he entered the building, Barun looked over his shoulder to check that he had not been followed. Satisfied that there was no one watching him, he knocked five times on the door. A burly man answered and quickly ushered him inside. He always found it fascinating seeing police officers wearing casual clothes. Barun would not have taken the captain for a wearer of bell-bottomed trousers, and he found it hard not to gawp in surprise as the man approached him.

'Very well done, Barun. We've got enough to make an arrest,' the captain said, pointing over to the large tape recorder that was sat between two broken sewing machines on a table.

The reels of the recorder were still spinning, and the young police officer operating it took off her headphones before giving Barun a thumbs-up.

Barun began to unbutton his shirt. 'I am glad to hear it, captain.'

'However, we will need to find her body if we are to take the case to trial. Pity he didn't let slip where he left her,' the captain said.

The wire was stuck to Barun's chest with several strips of tape, and he winced as he pulled the first strip off. 'I know where she is, captain. You'll find her in the attic. She is within a sack inside a leather trunk.'

The captain's eyes widened. 'How do you know that? I was listening in myself and heard no mention of that.'

'The girl told me herself. You see, I was lying to Rihaan when I said my Tamil isn't very good. Though I am nowhere near fluent, I did understand a majority of what she told me. By the way, you didn't happen to pick up her voice on the recording?'

The captain looked awkwardly down at his shoes. 'Actually, Barun, when you were in the cellar, we only heard your voice. We could hear you asking someone questions, but we couldn't make out anyone but you.'

Barun stopped what he was doing and stood motionless for a while as he thought to himself. 'I suppose it would have been too much to ask for some concrete evidence of the existence of spirits,' he said after a while. 'At least I may come closer to convincing you when you recover the body.'

'Even when we do, I still don't think I'll know what to make of any of this, Barun, but I am relieved we can put this swine away for the rest of his life. I must say, I'm shocked he's been keeping her in the same building that he sleeps in for all this time. He's a bigger monster than I first thought.'

'It would appear that he has been waiting for an opportune moment to drop the trunk in the nearest river,' Barun said. 'I am not a psychologist, though it does seem like he is a contradiction of a man. On the one hand, he is very cautious, yet at the same time he seems to enjoy the thrill of living life on the edge. I wouldn't be surprised if this is also part of the reason he has left her there.'

'He'll talk when we take him in. Most of the clever ones can't resist telling us how they fooled us.' The captain gestured to his officers. 'Surround the property. I'll be with you in two minutes.'

The captain's officers checked their pistols before swiftly leaving the building.

'Before you leave, captain, I want to let you know the reason why her spirit passed on to the other side,' Barun said. 'I promised her that her uncle would be brought to justice.'

'She was a troubled girl, though she certainly did not deserve what happened to her. I'll make sure Rihaan gets what's coming to him.' The captain gave a solemn nod. 'Goodbye, and thank you for your help.'

Once he was left alone, Barun idly ran his hand along one of the disused pieces of machinery then stared at the thick layer of dust on his fingers. He wiped his hand clean on his coat before he headed out into the night.

PERSONAL CORRESPONDENCES

Submission for the Journal of Psychology, 2012.

Note: The following correspondences were salvaged from the Harlow College archives after the 2004 server fire. Parapsychologist Barun Rai is listed as a guest lecturer for the years 1968 to 1979, and submitted much of his work for the archives. While little was accepted and the details of Rai's termination are now lost, these letters were found in a briefcase on the one shelf that remained untouched by the fire.

18th July 1969

Dear Sukhbir,

Please find enclosed the correspondence that you requested from me. I have also included copies of my own letters, the ones I sent to Professor Carter, as they will probably help you to understand the circumstances. Best of luck in your investigation.

Yours Faithfully,
Barun

29th May 1968

Dear Mister Rai,

My name is Professor Carter, and I will be taking charge of Professor Overton's department whilst he undergoes his knee operation. In all honesty, Mister Rai, the reason that I have contacted you is that I have several concerns regarding both your research and your methods. The evidence you have provided is essentially anecdotal, whilst the only recording you appear to have provided is poor in quality. What I find most disturbing is that it is quite evident that you believe the phenomena to be real.

I would like you, therefore, to shed some light on your recent research trips to New Orleans and Madrid. I look forward to your response.

Yours sincerely,
Professor K. Carter

9th June 1968

Dear Prof. Carter,

I am sorry to hear that you have reservations on my work. In this letter I hope to allay your concerns regarding my investigations by convincing you that my accounts are entirely genuine.

Firstly, I will recount the incident in Madrid. I found out about the woman by chance while I was attending a lecture in Bilbao. I was told there was an individual in the capital that was displaying behaviours which had perplexed all the physicians that had so far examined her. Unfortunately, it is difficult getting around Spain due to its current regime, though I was eventually given permission to travel to see her. By this stage, the situation had become so dire that the woman had a whole hospital wing to herself. The doctors had moved all the other patients due to the dangers she posed to them. I was shown scratches that she had made on walls using her bare hands, as well as a door that she had ripped from its hinges. Her belligerence towards the staff had intensified over time, and they avoided being in the same room as her whenever possible.

My first contact with her was through a barred window. She quickly began to tell me everything she knew about me. I was astonished by the details she gave of my life growing up in India, as she could not have possibly learned the information she divulged from anyone in the hospital for no one there had ever met me before that day. The whole time I was in her presence, I discerned a whisper coming from behind me. Whenever I tried to focus on this whispering, it would stop completely. Eventually, she became terribly aggressive towards me so I left her company.

With the medical professionals and psychologists out of ideas, I decided to call for the hospital chaplain. Returning to the woman alongside the chaplain, I witnessed a drastic change in her mood. There was fear in her eyes. The chaplain began to recite a prayer – the Prayer to Saint Michael, I believe – which caused her to wail. Fortunately, the spirit that was inside her was not strong-willed. The spirit vacated the woman's body, and the last I heard she was living happily in France working as a baker.

There was no happy conclusion, on the other hand, with the case in New Orleans. An old acquaintance of mine who was working as a private investigator phoned me late one night. I had barely answered when he handed the phone over to a young man who had recently migrated to America from Liberia. He told me a tale of how he had left his homeland in order to escape a mysterious creature that was following him. What piqued my interest was that other people had seen this creature. He had a name for this beast: a Tolokoshe. When I met him at the train station, I could tell that this was a man on the edge. He was nervy, flinching at almost every noise he heard. So from there we went to a quiet cafe where I devised a plan to catch this strange being. I had already heard of the African legend of the Tolokoshe and knew that a bite from one could prove fatal, and for this reason alone I decided I had to proceed with a high degree of caution. That said, the only way we could hope to stop it was to use the man it was stalking as bait. The creature tried to enter into his bedroom most nights via the window, so that night we left it unlocked and waited patiently. As you will have read in my report, I never got a clear sight of the Tolokoshe. All I saw in the darkness was a small creature with a set of sharp fangs.

Once it had entered through the window, I lit a branch that I had doused in oil and used it to corner the beast. As part of the trap we had propped a crate up against a wall, and we slammed it down once the Tolokoshe was in position. Only when we turned the crate over, the beastly thing had disappeared. There were some scratch marks in the floorboards, but except for them there was no other trace that the Tolokoshe had ever set foot in the room. I stayed in New Orleans for a further week, and in that time the creature paid no more visits to the young man. Of course, I could not hang around in the city forever, and so I left him a telephone number that he could contact me on before moving onto my next case. You will not find in my case notes that I heard six years later that the man sadly died in unusual circumstances. The postmortem concluded that he had died from a dog bite, yet the coroner's report conveniently ignored that he was in a locked room when he was found. According to a friend of his, he had begun to claim in the days following up to his death that he was once more being followed by the Tolokoshe.

In regard to evidence, I would be more than willing to supply you with a list of people that would corroborate my accounts. It is unfortunate that the technologies of today are not yet of a standard capable of recording definitive evidence of the existence of spirits and other paranormal beings. Admittedly, I agree that the recording you have listened to of the Madrid Affair is, as you say, poor in quality, though I can promise you that it is indeed genuine.

I hope that this letter goes some way to convincing you that my work is free from both conjecture or speculation. If you would like to know more about anything I have discussed, please feel free to contact me again.

Yours sincerely,
Barun Rai

19th June 1968

Dear Mister Rai,

I regret to inform you that I am unsatisfied by your attempt to rationalise your work to me. It is very much my opinion that all the theories you have put forward are completely devoid of rationality. Although I specifically questioned those two particular cases, I could quite have easily queried every single investigation that you have submitted to the university.

I read your case entitled "The Broadbank Incident" this morning. I do not live far from where this "incident" took place, and I have taken it upon myself to make travel arrangements to visit the area in question. It is my intention to compile my own report which I will present to the Vice-Chancellor. Should I find no signs of the phenomena that you claim is rife inside the former Broadbank Institute, I will be putting forward a recommendation that your association with the university comes to an end.

Yours Sincerely,
Professor K. Carter

26th June 1968

Dear Prof. Carter,

I have made several attempts to speak to you over the phone, and I can only hope that this letter reaches you before you depart. I implore you not to enter Broadbank. It may appear to you to be nothing but a derelict building; however, I can assure you there is more to Broadbank than meets the eye. The woods surrounding the building are home to a beast that, alas, I was unable to identify, but it is inside where the real dangers lie. A kanabhulo – a type of spirit rarely found in this continent – haunts the corridors and will attack the living indiscriminately. Never have I come across such a vicious spirit, one filled with utter hatred for everyone it sets eyes on. A team of experts and I attempted to cleanse the building of this threat; however, this kanabhulo was resistant to our efforts. No prayer, chant nor incantation had any effect whatsoever. Slashing the arm of one of our number, the kanabhulo became more and more enraged until we had no option but to leave for our own safety.

Against the wishes of others I returned to the accursed place alongside a gentleman called Oswald Mortagne. My companion was somewhat of an eccentric, claiming to be a member of the Knights Templar, though I have known few people more knowledgeable on the subject of the paranormal. Armed with steel, we attacked the kanabhulo head-on, and for a while it appeared as though we were going to defeat it once and for all. Just as Mortagne was about to deal the final blow, it bewitched him. He threw down his weapon and fled from the building leaving me alone with the monster. I continued to fight on, though I suffered a sharp blow across the head and once more had to withdraw from Broadbank. When I eventually reached a hospital I discovered the extent of my injuries. Two of my fingers had been broken, my right lung was collapsed and I had a severe concussion. My recovery was a slow progress. It was while I was in hospital that I discovered that no one had seen Mortagne since he fled Broadbank. He remains missing to this day.

Please, professor, do not go to that place.

Barun Rai

1st August 1968

Dear Barun,

I hope you are well. As I am fairly certain you are aware, I have been on recovery leave following my knee operation – that bit of shrapnel that's been rattling around since my days in Burma finally needed to be taken out – at an excellent hospital just outside Edinburgh. I would first like to confirm this: the university is happy with your work, and I have been given assurances that your position is secure. Professor Carter is a very bright fellow, but he was far too rash to suggest that your role was under threat.

This leads me to the next matter that I must bring up. The professor travelled from his home to East Anglia on 21st June. Colleagues of the professor have vouched that they saw him pay a visit to his office five days later and since then there have been no further sightings of him. Peculiarly, one of the people who saw him claimed that someone was following close behind him, though they did not get a proper look of this individual. The professor's sister informed me that she spoke to him over the phone around this time, and he mumbled to her something about needing to travel to South Asia. No explanation was given as to why he felt compelled to leave the country without telling his employers other than that someone had ordered him to go.

We recovered your letters from his desk, and from what I have gathered he was visiting East Anglia because he wanted to see Broadbank for himself. Discussions have taken place whether faculty members should visit the place on the off chance that they can find clues regarding Professor Carter's disappearance. You will be happy to know that I convinced my colleagues that travelling to Broadbank would be an altogether unnecessary idea.

Please can you call in on me when you get a chance, old friend, as I would like to confer with you in person on this matter. I will be back on campus from tomorrow. Anyway, let us hope that all this fuss is for nothing and the good professor turns up safe and sound.

Kindest regards,
Professor Henry Overton

10:38, 04/08/12

To: a.overton@hc.ac.uk

From: Journal of Psychology

Subject: Your Submission

Dear Mr. Overton,

The Journal of Psychology is grateful for your submission. We are sorry to report that we will not be accepting your submission 'A History of Parapsychology at Harlow College'. Please do not let this deter you from future submission.

Many thanks,
The Journal of Psychology.

BARUN RAI AND THE NIGHTMARE'S HAND

coming soon

www.ingramcontent.com/pod-product-compliance
Lightning Source LLC
La Vergne TN
LVHW091204150826
845672LV00005B/1243

* 9 7 9 8 8 8 9 0 9 9 9 0 1 *